MARGARET MAHY

THE
GREATEST SHOW
OFF EARTH

Illustrated by Wendy Smith

PUFFIN BOOKS

To Patricia

PUFFIN BOOKS

Published by the Penguin Group
Penguin Books Ltd, 27 Wrights Lane, London W8 5TZ, England
Penguin Books USA Inc., 375 Hudson Street, New York, New York 10014, USA
Penguin Books Australia Ltd, Ringwood, Victoria, Australia
Penguin Books Canada Ltd, 10 Alcorn Avenue, Toronto, Ontario, Canada M4V 3B2
Penguin Books (NZ) Ltd, 182–190 Wairau Road, Auckland 10, New Zealand

Penguin Books Ltd, Registered Offices: Harmondsworth, Middlesex, England

First published by Hamish Hamilton Ltd 1994
Published in Puffin Books 1996
1 3 5 7 9 10 8 6 4 2

A Vanessa Hamilton Book

CONTENTS

PART ONE

PART TWO

PART THREE

PART FOUR

Part One

1

A Birthday Surprise

'Happy birthday to me,' sang Delphinium, dreaming of cake and candles as she sang. Though she was sitting in a roomful of sensitive computers, she had to sing her own Happy Birthday to herself, for not one computer was programmed to sing this fine old song to her. And, though she was the cleverest calculator on Space Station Vulnik (besides being the only girl), she did not have the merest ghost of an idea that she was singing her way into an adventure story.

'Happy birthday to me,' she chanted loudly, kicking her heels in time to the song.

A stern voice came thundering out of a little grille, right next to her ear – the voice of Flinders, the Space Station Vulnik snoopervisor, snooping as usual. He was sitting back comfortably, watching screens that showed him every single curve and corner of the space station. As he himself hadn't bothered to celebrate a birthday in years, he didn't see why anyone else should.

'Stop that singing at once!' he commanded. 'You will raise the fun level, and too much fun is dangerous for all of us. Remember what happened to your parents!'

'That wasn't because of fun,' argued Delphinium. 'They vanished during an explosion. They were blown into dust particles.'

'Well then, remember what happened to that wretched Wonder Show!' cried Flinders quickly. 'There was certainly too much fun going on there. That Wonder Show popped out of nowhere and began working its way round the edge of the known universe, having a good time all the way. Most dangerous! But would they listen to our sensible warnings? No! And now they've vanished. Fizz! Phutt! So, think of the Wonder Show and shut up at once.'

Delphinium thought of the Wonder Show, stopped singing, and groaned quietly instead.

'That's better,' said Flinders in a kinder voice, for groaning and moaning were all encouraged on Space Station Vulnik. 'Now, remember the sacred space station rules! No joking! No singing! Sit still, feeling weary, dreary and smeary, and, above all, stare hard at your screen without blinking – just in case.'

Though Delphinium tried to sit still, she twitched with impatience under her dark blue overall. 'It's my birthday,' she thought, 'and I'm ten, which is *double numbers*. But here I am, stuck in front of a screen (just as usual), on level seven of Space Station Vulnik (just as usual). And nobody turning ten, not even a space weevil, should have to feel merely usual.'

She knew that in other parts of the universe, other children – children whose parents *hadn't* been blown to cosmic dust in a giant explosion – were actually allowed to *enjoy* their birthdays.

'Birthdays are meant to be glorious,' she whispered rebelliously, 'and a *tenth* birthday should be gloriously glorious.' Then, daringly, she glanced sideways at a particular button . . . the red alarm button, with the word DANGER engraved on it. Her fingers twitched with wicked excitement.

2

The Red DANGER Button

Delphinium was forbidden to touch this red DANGER button, or even to look at it for more than a second at a time. All the same, she suddenly felt certain that pressing the DANGER button would provide a moment of glory. 'That's what I want for my birthday,' she suddenly thought, running her fingers through her mouse-coloured hair just to keep them busy. 'A moment of glory!'

She imagined a finger – *her* finger – landing fiercely on the red button. All levels of Space Station Vulnik would scream with sirens and shriek with alarms. Everyone would panic. Even the team of commandos down on level ten would be stricken with fear, but she – she, Delphinium, the wonder-girl calculator – would instantly come up with a plan (she didn't know what), that would save everyone on the whole space station. Saving lives (along with a whole lot of highly expensive computers) felt as if it would be enormous glory, and good fun, too.

Dreaming of fun and glory, Delphinium twiddled her long, lively fingers over the red DANGER button.

'I see you!' growled Flinders through the grille, snooping again. 'Stop it at once! Twiddling is only allowed in R & R.'

R & R stood for rest and recreation, but it was mostly rest and not much recreation, for all fun was strictly forbidden on Space Station Vulnik. This was no problem for computers which never, ever longed to twiddle fingers over their own DANGER buttons, or to have glorious moments. Not only that, they were expensive technology, whereas Delphinium had cost Space Station Vulnik nothing at all.

Once upon a time, back when she was not much more than a baby, something dangerous and exciting had happened to Delphinium. After the great Dwodian Flare-up (the explosion in which her parents, along with Molly, her nanny, had been blown into cosmic dust), Delphinium had been found in a wastepaper basket among the ruins of the planet Dwode. Tests showed she was quite unharmed, but they also

proved that she was going to be a brilliant
calculator. So, almost at once, she was given
special calculating work on level seven of Space
Station Vulnik, and since then nothing interest-
ing had ever been allowed to happen to her.

'Ten years old!' thought Delphinium gloomily. 'One year for every finger . . . and not even
allowed to twiddle my fingers over the
DANGER button! Life is passing me by.'

3

A Library Prances By

Life wasn't all that was passing her by at that moment. Jason Jones, the only other young person on Space Station Vulnik, happened to be prancing past. Nose in the air – utterly easy for someone with an inquisitive, turned-up, librarian-ish nose like his – Jason shot past, shining slightly, for his black, library overall was covered with luminous pictures copied from ancient books. He also wore glowing-pink sneakers with yellow laces. Delphinium wished for a moment that she was a library and allowed to wear illustrated clothes.

'Bookworm!' she hissed at his back, jealous of his shining illustrations and cheerful prancing. 'You're not invited to *my* birthday! Ha ha ha ha!'

'Cack-cack calculator!' he cried over his shoulder, as he jumped on to the strip of moving carpet which whisked him towards the door. 'I wouldn't come anyway.'

Then he was whooshed away under posters offering huge rewards to anyone who found the missing Wonder Show, or caught the space pirate Bamba Caramba and his desperate crew. Over these posters an electronic display flashed on and off bathing them in lurid light. *ACROPOLA! ACROPOLA! ACROPOLA!* it read in big, green, dripping, capital letters. This was to remind everyone on Space Station Vulnik just what they were supposed to be watching out for. This was why there was a red DANGER button beside Delphinium's screen.

4

Acropola! Acropola! Acropola!

The Acropola were great, green, mysterious
aliens, shaped like slugs but swift as serpents,
sliming their way around the edge of the known
universe. When they had first appeared (from
somewhere out in the *un*known universe), commandos from hundreds of frontier space stations
had rushed out with ray guns and blasted them
to twenty-eight million smithereens. The commandos felt sure they had won, and immediately began grinning and slapping one another
on the back. But, before they had finished the
grinning and back-slapping, every single smithereen started to seethe and swell, and in no
time at all there were twenty-eight million times
more Acropola on the edge of the known universe than there had been ten minutes earlier.
Blasting the Acropola to smithereens had turned

out to be the sort of terrible mistake that space commandos sometimes make. Anyhow, the twenty-eight million Acropola (plus a few extra) began to slime their way forward, driving the commandos before them. And, little by little, they had been sliming onward ever since.

The Acropola lived on fun-energy. Across space their fun detectors were always alert for laughter and singing. They made an instant bee-line, or rather, Acropola-line, for any place where people were enjoying themselves. In they slimed, like giant space leeches, sucking up every little bit of fun-energy. And then, once all the fun was sucked away, they would start moaning, as if in terrible pain, and set off, looking for more fun to absorb, leaving nothing but deep misery, and even deeper darkness, behind them. That's why all fun levels were kept extremely low on Space Station Vulnik. Nobody wanted to attract the Acropola.

Delphinium rather wished Jason had hung around a little longer, for she had thought of other good, insulting names to call him. But hanging around was not allowed by the snooper-visors on Space Station Vulnik. 'And anyhow, I might have enjoyed name-calling a bit too much,' she thought with a sigh.

And then, just as she was staring gloomily into the circle of her screen, thinking about birthdays, and longing for a glorious moment, something actually happened at last. Something astounding! Something *incredible*! In the exact middle of that round screen a little light no bigger than the head of a pin seemed to flick *on* then *off*, then *on* again. Delphinium had received a birthday present, after all. Indeed, just for a moment, she thought that the unknown universe was looking back at her from the middle of her screen and was actually winking at her.

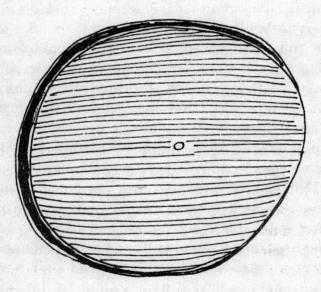

5

A Mysterious UFO

A UFO!

Delphinium did not hesitate. At last! At last! Her moment of glory had arrived, and not before time. Out shot her finger. No more twiddling! It pressed hard on the red DANGER button.

Bells rang! Sirens wailed! Every alarm system on Space Station Vulnik leaped to life. Up on level one, scientists scrambled to their screens and peered into them anxiously. Down on level ten, a team of trained commandos stopped picking their teeth (or beaks or fangs, depending on which planet they had come from) while filling in time playing boring games of interspace poker. As one supremely well-trained commando, they sprang to their toes (or claws), flexed every single muscle three times, ran to snatch up their proton cannons, then moved to action stations. All over Space Station Vulnik computers peeped and whistled. Librarians gabbled and scientists gobbled. Everyone was electrified.

Well, not *quite* everyone. There was actually one person (someone who hasn't come into the story so far) who merely moaned impatiently at the sound of the DANGER sirens. This was partly because he was a coward and detested all dangers, even very small ones, and partly because he had been looking forward to a secret treat, and did not want to share any of it with anyone else.

6

A Cowardly Broom-master

This person, moaning over the bells and alarms, was the space station janitor, someone who had risen, through years of precision sweeping and polishing, to the rank of broom-master. He came from Ophidia, a planet well known for its great variety of smells. Some were tasty and some were terrible. Anyhow, the people who settled on Ophidia had evolved, over thousands of years, into enormously tall, greenish people with two noses – one nose for good smells and one for bad. These noses were commonly known as the aroma-comber and the stinker-drinker. All over the universe, Ophidians were at work, using their noses to the full.

But though they were highly professional sniffers and could tell at one sniff if your mother had been tidying your wardrobe while you were downstairs stealing biscuits, or if your teacher was tiptoeing down the school corridor, Ophidians were all hopeless cowards, and the Station Vulnik janitor was the most cowardly of them all. He had started off wanting to be captain of a space ship, but then he found that even vacuum cleaners terrified him. It turned out that he was much happier pedalling the Station Vulnik broom-machine, which he did enormously well.

'The pay isn't great,' he used to say, 'but there's more to life than money.' So, when this janitor heard alarm bells ringing, he didn't think, 'Oh good! Danger!' as a commando or a space-ship pilot would have done. Instead, he thought, 'Something smells funny, and it isn't just the commandos' dirty socks and combat boots. I'm getting out of here.'

Here was the R & R galley where the janitor was making himself delicious glop sandwiches, and preparing to watch the video of episode one million of a fabulous soap opera, *Intergalactic Hospital*. He had had this video smuggled on to Space Station Vulnik in a shipment of floor polish, for he knew that in this episode the beautiful nurse Nydia was to marry, at long last, handsome Captain Iro whom she had nursed through a frightful attack of wambles. *But* (and this was the big problem) could two such different life forms find happiness together? *He* was a lizard-man from the planet Gecko, while *she* was composed largely of intelligent light particles, and travelled so fast that time slowed down around her. For instance, if she went down to the shop for a loaf of bread and came back in what seemed to her to be five minutes, she would find everyone else in the hospital had aged twenty years. It was a heart-breaking problem.

Anyhow, what with the millionth episode of *Intergalactic Hospital* and the glop sandwiches, this particular janitor, known as the Mangold, was planning to enjoy himself much more than he was supposed to. But, having two sensitive noses, Ophidians soon sniff their way into every little corner of any place they happen to be,

and this janitor knew of one particular, special, insulated television booth in which rising fun levels could not possibly be detected. All around him bells were still ringing and sirens still screaming. Feet pounded (and claws scrabbled) past the galley. Commandos shouted to each other, giving short, savage, gurgling cries. But nothing, not even a UFO, was going to stop the Mangold watching *Intergalactic Hospital*.

Grabbing his plate of glop sandwiches and his video, he raced out of the galley, leaped on to the moving carpet, turned up the speed to 10, and was whisked away at great speed.

Whoooosh! See? There he goes, out he goes . . . out at the end of the chapter, thinking he has managed to free himself from the story. Little does he know that this story is not an easy one to escape from. Little does he know that it has many surprises still in store for him.

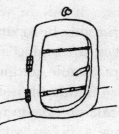

7

Ranting, Raving and Roaring

Meanwhile, Delphinium was absolutely enraptured with her moment of glory. But it didn't last very long. Flinders shot out of his snoopervisor's chair, to snoop over her shoulder.

'Is it . . . is it the Acropola?'

Delphinium pressed her telescope key. Her screen immediately magnified the white worm. Flinders cried out aloud at what he now saw. Even the more advanced computers whirred with astonishment.

'A flying castle,' Flinders murmured. 'Look at all its banners! But what's it doing here? Where has it come from? Why is it upside down? We need someone with a huge brain to work this one out.'

'My brain's growing bigger every minute,' promised Delphinium cheerfully, looking forward to being extremely glorious for the rest of the day.

But Flinders did something dreadful.

'Here, shift over,' he said. Taking her arm as if it were a mere handle, he pulled her out of her chair and slid into Station 7037 himself. Then he began talking into Delphinium's intercom in special space-station talk.

'Section Otter-Antelope. Emergency status confirmed. Code Elephant. Focus on Sector Zebra and co-ordinate reports . . .' and so on.

Delphinium was simply furious. That flying castle was *her* discovery. Not only that, it was *her* birthday. Yet, right in the middle of a moment of glory, she had been tossed aside like the empty wrapper of a crambo bar. She felt that if she didn't rant and roar and rave, she might explode. Of course, all explosions were forbidden on Space Station Vulnik, particularly after the great Dwodian Flare-up, but then roaring, ranting and raving were all forbidden as well, just in case people enjoyed them too much. Nobody was allowed to do anything which might attract the Acropola's attention.

Bursting with fury, Delphinium leaped on to the moving carpet and was whooshed towards the door. Nobody even noticed her leaving. Not one computer shouted, 'Attention! Delphinium, the brilliant discoverer of this UFO, is leaving us.' Flinders did not once cry, 'Wait, Delphinium! We can't possibly manage without you.'

But, as the moving carpet swept her towards the anti-grav-whizz-pole which ran from level to level right through the middle of Space Station Vulnik, Delphinium suddenly noticed the door of the nearest emergency exit. She had seen this door many times before, but this time there was something different about it. What could it be? Of course! The red light in the middle had changed to bright green. Pushing the DANGER button had triggered all emergency doors, and prepared all emergency skip-ships in case the crew of Space Station Vulnik needed to get away quickly. That emergency exit marked the very place where a poor, disappointed calculator would be able to roar and rant and rave to her heart's content. Leaping off the moving carpet, Delphinium swung the emergency door open and vanished beyond it.

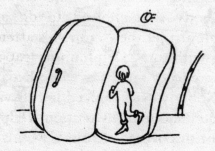

8

Delphinium is Fantabulously Clever

Once in the emergency exit bay, Delphinium roared and ranted and raved, kicking her legs and waving her arms like propellers for about five minutes. All that exercise made her hungry. When she stopped roaring, ranting and raving, she found she was starving.

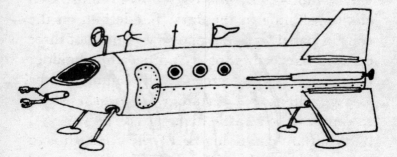

There, in front of her, was a life-boat . . . a special skip-ship called *Dragonfly* . . . and Delphinium knew that there were cupboards of emergency rations on board all life-boats. Nobody would miss a packet of delicious shredded skudge, a glop pie or a crambo bar or two.

The sound-proof, space-proof, and possibly even Acropola-proof sliding door of *Dragonfly* always unlocked itself during an emergency. Delphinium opened it easily. But what was this? The cabin should have been empty, but a strange, luminous glow was shifting around it. A mysterious shadow moved on the curved wall. Horrakapotchkin! Had *Dragonfly* been taken over by the Acropola? No! That shadow had a turned-up nose! No doubt about it, it was none other than Jason Jones, the walking library. And there he was, sitting behind the control panel, peering into a navigational screen, booming to himself like a laser cannon. The luminous glow was caused by his illustrated elothes, shining in the dark. Beside him on the control panel were the plastic wrappers of three crambo bars, all empty. And over his shoulder on the navigation screen, Delphinium saw he was goggling at a certain white worm which she knew to be a castle flying upside down.

'What are you doing here?' she cried, though it was obvious the greedy pig of a library had

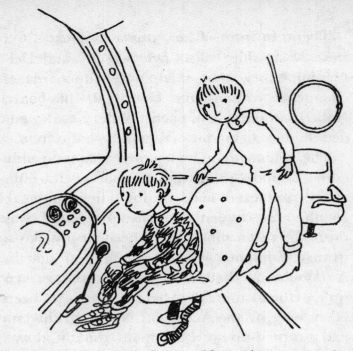

been *having secret fun*, wolfing down crambo
bars, while pretending to be king of the commandos. Jason jumped.

'Nothing,' he said quickly, blushing deeply so
that his face (and particularly his nose) turned
shocking pink. 'I wanted to see what was going
on, so I hid in here,' he cried defiantly.

'They threw me out,' said Delphinium gloomily. 'And *I* was the one who first saw the flying
castle. *I* was the one who pressed the DANGER
button.'

'You? You pressed the DANGER button?'
cried Jason. His own fingers twitched, and a

faint greenness (a sure sign of envy) crept over his pink face. 'What did it feel like?'

'Awesome!' said Delphinium. 'It was a moment of real glory. But it was much too short. I wanted a moment of glory that would last about five years. Right now this minute they'll be having urgent conferences and consultations, and then they'll probably send out a scout-ship full of commandos. They won't take me, the first finder, though, mind you, *I* could plot a course to that flying castle as quickly as any old computer.'

'Could you?' asked Jason, turning even greener.

Having a library look at her so greenly was almost as good as another moment of glory – only a small one, but a lot better than nothing.

'Simple-pimple!' said Delphinium. 'Look! They'll whoosh off in skip-ships like this one, and take short cuts through a special sort of space called hyperspace. You can't see hyperspace, but people with the most fantabulous skill (which is what *I* just happen to have) can calculate their way into it.'

And then, dying to show Jason just how fantabulously skilful she was, Delphinium started to calculate. Numbers began a mysterious dance through her head. Some of them spun alone, while others chose partners with which to spin. Some added themselves up and turned into entirely different figures. Others multiplied themselves *by* themselves. One group of dancing numbers stood for Space Station Vulnik, while others pinpointed the flying castle. The number dance was too big and mysterious for Delphinium to understand completely. As usual, though, she was amazed by its beauty. Quickly, she punched in the pattern of part of the dance on the navigational keyboard. A curious line, like a crooked rainbow, crept across the screen.

'There!' she said at last. 'That's how we would get to the flying castle in about half an hour. We would skip from *there* to *there* to *THERE*, even closer to the edge of the known universe than where we are now – almost into the unknown universe! Just press that red button marked IF ONLY . . . and Whoooosh! We're off.'

9

Whoooosh!

'IF ONLY ...' repeated Jason dreamily. 'It sounds like part of a story. You know! If only *we* could have an exciting adventure. If only *we* could solve the mystery of the flying castle. If only *we* could catch the notorious space pirate, Bamba Caramba, or find the lost Wonder Show. Then we would win enormous rewards from the Intergalactic Banking system, and be rich enough to go in any direction we wanted to.'

'I know,' said Delphinium, amazed to find that Jason dreamed *if only* dreams just as she did. 'If only *we* could find a way to conquer the Acropola. If only everyone understood how really fantabulous we are! But *this* IF ONLY means "Initiate Fusion Only". It whoooshes the skip-ship off into outer space.'

A strange look crept across Jason's face.

33

'You mean, this button here would whoosh us away?' he asked, twiddling his fingers over the red IF ONLY button, and Delphinium suddenly remembered the green envy that had crept over his pink face only a moment earlier. Jason was jealous of her moment of glory. He wanted to have one of his own.

'Don't!' she yelled, but it was too late. Jason's finger shot out and pressed down on the red IF ONLY button.

Whooosh!

An enormous *Whoooosh!*

Fusion had been initiated, and now there was nothing either of them could do to stop it. Huge space-proof doors in the side of Space Station Vulnik slid open.

Whooosh and *Whooosh* again! The good skip-ship *Dragonfly* skipped obediently into infinite space, and Jason and Delphinium had no choice but to skip along with it.

WHOOSH!

10

An Angry Broom-master

Jason and Delphinium immediately began screaming at one another.

'Turn it round! Skip it backwards!' yelled Jason.

'I'm not a pilot. I don't know how to, you stupid library,' shouted Delphinium, wildly pressing command keys left, right and centre. Lights flashed on and off. Their chairs shot up-down-up-down, then spun madly round and round. The skip-ship radio blared out a trumpet fanfare, before switching itself off. Unknown electronic machinery went *Peep-peep-peep* and *Boing! Boing!* But nothing worked. *Dragonfly* whooshed busily onwards. The quartz glass windows suddenly blazed with stars.

'Are we really going to that flying castle?' wailed Jason.

'Yes,' cried Delphinium. 'And I'm not a navigator, only a calculator. When we get there we'll probably smash right into it.'

She stared helplessly at the control panel, and saw, over to one side where it was hard to reach, a small glittering key with a label on it. *Program Delete*, said the label. Perhaps it would wipe out the whole fatal, navigational program she had accidentally set in place while showing off to Jason Jones. By now, Delphinium had pressed so many buttons and keys that one more didn't seem to matter. She pressed *Program Delete*.

From somewhere behind them, there was a roar of anguish. It sounded faint and far away, like an echo from the unknown universe. There was no doubt about it, that anguish was the exact anguish of a soul in torment. A sound-proof door that neither of them had noticed before burst open, and an enormous figure, wearing a helmet – with wires and plugs dangling from it – squeezed into the cockpit.

'Who's wiped my episode one million? Zub-nasherbakk! There I was, lying back in the skip-ship video unit, plugged into every living, poignant moment of it, and I was nearly deleted, too.'

Delphinium and Jason stared at the creature. He was seven feet tall and wore a bright pink vest and matching tights. A large broom-master's medal was pinned in the centre of his pink chest where nobody could possibly miss it. Engraved on the medal, in clear letters, was the broom-masters' motto *New Brooms Sweep Clean*. Whoever he was . . . he was obviously Ophidian. Green feathers hung from under his helmet, and smaller, softer feathers grew down his neck and over the backs of his hands. He had purple eyes and two noses.

'I didn't mean to wipe your noses . . . I mean your program,' stammered Delphinium, horribly confused. 'I was trying to delete something else.'

'We're on our way to crash into the flying castle,' wailed Jason, sounding just as terrified as if he had been an Ophidian himself.

The creature's face immediately wrinkled with shock.

'What flying castle?' he gasped.

'A flying castle has suddenly popped out of the unknown universe, and a state of alert has been called,' Delphinium explained quickly, hoping to drive lost episode one million from his mind.

'And *she's* programmed us to take short cuts through hyperspace and then crash into the flying castle,' yelled Jason, pointing at Delphinium.

'Don't tell tales,' Delphinium snapped at him.

'Tales are there to be told, and libraries are there to tell them,' argued Jason, still pointing at her. '*She* pressed the red DANGER button.'

'But *he* pressed the red IF ONLY button!' shouted Delphinium, pointing back. Calculators could tell tales, too. 'Fusion was initiated and here we are, whizzing through space with no pilot.'

'Your luck's in,' mumbled the creature in front of them. 'I just happen to be the most utterly careful pilot on Space Station Vulnik. Not that I've actually *flown* anything before, but I know all about it from pictures in books. By the way, I'm the Mangold.'

For the second time that day, Delphinium was lightly tossed out of her seat as the Mangold squeezed himself into it. But one glance at the screen and he let out a roar of dismay.

'What's this?' he cried. 'You fool! You've pressed too many keys. You've jammed the command program. Now, we'll *have* to go all the way out to this flying castle of yours before we're able to turn round and come back aga 1. Ahhhr! We're doomed!'

Just for a moment, Delphinium shivered. Here she was, trapped in an adventure story, shut in a skip-ship (probably a doomed one) not only with a tale-telling library whose inquisitive nose turned up, but with a seven-foot coward as well whose two noses both drooped down.

But then a shiver ran through the skip-ship, a shiver of light, and a shiver of something stranger than light. What they were all feeling was a shiver of time.

'Oh, sikkakkerblam!' yelled the Mangold, shouting a terrible Ophidian oath. 'The ship has just skipped for the first time. Off we go to another part of the edge of the known universe. Please note all seat belt signs are now off. You may move about the cabin, but don't smoke, smoulder or breathe fire.'

11

Hyperspace

As the ship skipped, Delphinium had a moment of time-sickness which made her queasy. Then the shiver passed. She and Jason slumped back into their seats, gurgling like plug holes, while the Mangold looked as if he might either be melting or moulting, or possibly both. 'All I wanted was a crambo bar,' thought Delphinium, 'and here I am, gurgling and goggling in outer space.'

'The stars have all gone,' said Jason in a wondering voice. 'What's that silver milk filling all the windows?'

'That's hyperspace,' explained Delphinium. 'I told you about it . . . a space with more than four dimensions,' she added, in a slow, kind voice as if speaking to a mere pot plant.

'Everyone knows that,' said Jason scornfully.

'Well, you didn't know,' Delphinium cried, just as scornfully. 'A library only knows words, not meanings.'

'Ha! Ha! You're not so smart! The words and their meanings are part of the same thing,' said Jason. He looked at her curiously. 'How did you come to be a calculator?' he asked her.

It was the first time that anyone had actually asked Delphinium a question about herself. She brightened up immediately.

'I'll tell you my life story,' she offered eagerly.

'No! Hang on! I'll tell you mine,' cried Jason. 'I'm not just a library. I'm an orphan.'

'So am I!' Delphinium exclaimed. 'I've been an orphan, and a calculator, too, for almost as long as I can remember. But before I came here I had a lot of adventures, and I can remember bits of them. I'll tell you about them.'

'No, let *me* tell *you*!' said Jason.

The Mangold slumped down in his seat with the expression of an Ophidian prepared to hear the worst.

12

Life Story One

'My parents were explorers and they fell into the crater of the volcano Poppaloo a few months after I was born,' said Jason. 'I was left with my big brother, Brockley.'

'You were lucky to have a big brother,' said Delphinium, who often wished she had had a few brothers and sisters.

'But Brockley wanted to be big without actually having to be a brother,' said Jason. 'He longed to be old enough to shave and to live a dashing, dangerous life. He wanted to fall in love with stormy, beautiful women (the taller the better), and he hated having to look after a baby. I did my best to grow quickly but I couldn't grow fast enough for Brockley. Anyway, when I was four years old . . .'

'*I* was three when *my* adventures really began,' said Delphinium. 'I turned three, exactly seven years ago today, on the day of the great Dwodian Flare-up when my parents and my nanny were all exploded into cosmic dust.'

'*I'm* telling first,' cried Jason. 'I'm eleven. I'm older than you and the oldest goes first. Listen! My brother Brockley was big, all right – big enough to look at himself in the mirror and count any whiskers he saw coming through. But, as big brothers go, he was a *short* big brother. Oh, he did his best to stretch himself (for instance he was the leader of a low-gravity gymnastic team), but I think I would have caught up with him if I had only had a chance. Every evening he would invite his whole gymnastic team around. After practising their tricks, they would read a lot of stories to one another, and every story they read was about space pirates. I must say I grew rather bored with pirates, pirates, pirates – night after night. Even when I was a mere four-year-old I was already planning to become a librarian because not many pirates come into libraries. And then something terrible happened. There was a knock on the door. The superintendent of the Explorers' Orphanage had called in to collect me. "But we never ever take orphans who have begun shaving!" said the superintendent,

frowning as he looked Brockley up and down. "You'll have to get a job. We'll find work for you as a space station janitor, driving a broom-machine."

"Never," cried Brockley. "I shall grow a beard, and live a wicked life with lots and lots of adventures. The hour has come. Follow me!" he shouted to his friends. And off he ran out of the door, followed by all his friends. I was not only fatherless and motherless, but brotherless, too. Isn't that one of the saddest stories you've ever heard? I can't think why you're not crying more.'

'I'm not crying at all,' said Delphinium. 'You're not crying yourself, and it actually happened to you.'

'I'm used to the sadness by now,' said Jason, patting the Mangold on the back, for the Mangold was sobbing and snuffling enough for several people. 'Cheer up! It was all a long time ago.'

'I'm crying because your brother didn't want to drive a broom-machine,' mumbled the Mangold. 'Insulting broom-machines makes me very angry, and if I grow angry I might do something accidently brave, so I make myself cry as quickly as I can. There's nothing that frightens an Ophidian more than the thought of being brave by accident.'

13

Life Story Two

'Well, I knew someone who hated broom-machines, too,' said Delphinium, 'and that was my nanny. You see, my parents were calculators like me (only not as fantabulous). They worked in a special, secret, sealed, stone room in the middle of the Acropola Research Centre on the Planet Dwode, which is a few light-years further around the edge of the known universe.'

'What were they doing there?' asked Jason. 'Why was the stone room sealed?'

'Because Acropola research is so dangerous,' said Delphinium. 'My parents had a boxful of rare Acropola eggs and those eggs had to be kept exceptionally safe, first in a special blue box with temperature controls, and then in a double-locked stone room which nobody else was allowed to enter. It was guarded by commandos, and the only way in was across a narrow plank stretched over a deep gully. Every morning, when my parents went in to do their work, they had to double-lock the door after them, then put on masks, and run sensitive, electronic tape over the cracks around the doors and windows ... or that's what Flinders tells me, anyway. Not only that, next door in the cafeteria, they had two refrigerators, one of them full of deep-frozen Acropola smithereens. They were trying to find a way to stop a smithereen turning back into a full-grown Acropola.

'My nanny was called Molly,' Delphinium continued, 'and she was particularly tall and stormy for a nanny. She used to be polite

enough when my parents were around, but once they had left for work, she would stamp and throw things, complaining bitterly about having to clean up after scientists. She especially hated using the broom-machines.' (The Mangold suddenly began sobbing and snuffling so loudly, that Delphinium had to raise her voice a little bit in order to make herself heard.) 'The thing was, Molly didn't really like children, and had only taken the job as nanny because she thought it would be very grand to be working on an important research planet like Dwode. No sooner had the door closed behind my mother and father than she used to tie me to the table with her dressing-gown cord, and spend hours posing in front of the mirror, trying out different, important voices. "A beautiful woman like you should be Q of the U," she used to say.'

'Q of the U?' cried Jason frowning. 'What's that?'

'I don't know,' Delphinium explained. 'She used to dye her hair all sorts of colours, purple or pink, and back-comb it into a crest and walk around in high-heeled boots ... anything to make herself even taller. But when the space pirates attacked, she deserted me at once.'

'Space pirates!' said Jason. 'Isn't it strange that both our stories have pirates in them?'

'But your brother and his gang were only *pretend* pirates,' cried Delphinium. 'My lot were real. I'll never forget the morning they attacked because it was my third birthday and I had just been given a wonderful birthday present. My first computer! Not that Molly let me play with it. Oh, no! She gave me a rubber duck that squeaked if you squeezed it. "That's what babies should play with," she said. "Leave computers to beautiful, tall people who understand such things." Then she began practising with it herself. Suddenly, the alarm went off. We were being invaded. The thud of feet (and hooves, too, because Flinders tells me some of the pirates came from very peculiar planets) sounded in the passage outside. Molly didn't do a thing to rescue me. She snatched up my computer, and jumped straight into the packing case in which it had just arrived, burrowing under the straw. I was left to save myself. I can just remember crawling into the wastepaper basket. All the same, Molly had made a mistake. When the pirates came rushing into the room shouting, "Yo! Ho! Ho!" and other pirate cries, two of them noticed the packing case.

'"There's something valuable packed in here," they cried, snatching it up, Molly and all, and running off with it. "If it's packed in straw," I heard them crying, "it must be because

there's something precious hidden inside it."
When they reached the stone room where my
parents were doing their secret Acropola research, the pirates quickly overcame the guards,
and tried to break down the door. What they
didn't realize was that Acropola eggs were completely top secret. If anyone tried opening that
sealed door without pressing in the secret code,
the room was programmed to explode.'

'Explode!' cried Jason, looking impressed at
last.

'And it did explode!' Delphinium yelled, fling-
ing her arms wide and leaping into the air to
give an impression of the explosion. 'That was
the great Dwodian Flare-up. It could be seen
from the Cubby Flubby nebula. The stone
room, my parents, the pirates, and Molly in the
packing case, along with my birthday present,
the computer, just vanished. Pages and pages
and pages of scorched notes were fluttering in
orbit around nearby planets for years afterwards.

'The rare Acropola eggs vanished, too; the
fridge in the cafeteria next door burst open,
throwing out the Acropola smithereens which
immediately defrosted in the intense heat of the
explosion. Ten minutes later, fully grown
Acropola were sliming all over what was left of
Dwode. The commandos had to get out as soon

as possible, but as they rushed to their space ship, one of them happened to notice a waste-paper basket bobbing about in the waves on the edge of the beach. He snatched it up, and there inside was a dear little girl. She was smiling up at him and counting on her fingers, since her birthday computer had been taken away from her by a faithless nanny.'

'Was that girl *you*?' cried Jason, screwing up his face as if the thought of Delphinium being a dear little girl was harder to believe than anything else in her life story.

'It *was*,' Delphinium said for she was telling a true story and did not want to spoil it with modesty. 'So here I am . . . I mean, there I was . . . an orphan working on Space Station Vulnik, instead of eating birthday cake and having fun – which I would be doing right now, if it hadn't been for the Acropola, wicked Molly, pirates and the explosion.'

'If my brother hadn't disappeared like that I expect I'd be helping to run the interplanetary library space ship,' sighed Jason. 'I'd be taking books from planet to planet and having adventures out among the stars.'

'Mind you, when you come to think of it, that's what we're doing now,' Delphinium pointed out. 'Having an adventure, I mean.'

'I suppose we are,' said Jason, sounding

surprised. 'I thought all this was an accident, but it feels adventurous. Hey! Perhaps *adventure* is just another word for *accident*.'

'Accidents or adventures . . . no one on Space Station Vulnik is allowed to have either of them,' groaned Delphinium.

The sound of sobbing bubbled up beside her. The Mangold was weeping.

'Let me tell you *my* life story,' he said. 'It's unbearably pathetic.'

They could tell he would snuffle all the way through any story he told, and two-nosed snuffling is a particularly irritating sound effect to have to endure. Delphinium looked around desperately. But Jason just smiled and said something extremely mysterious.

'Knock! Knock!'

Delphinium stared at him blankly, and the Mangold stopped snuffling.

'What do you mean, "Knock! Knock!"?' Delphinium asked.

'You have to say, "Who's there?"' Jason told her. 'Go on! Say it! You'll love this.'

'Who's there?' Delphinium said, humouring him.

'Zombie!' cried Jason. He seemed to be waiting for something. Delphinium shrugged her shoulders, staring at him even more blankly than before.

'You have to say "Zombie who?"' he explained impatiently.

'Zombie who?' asked Delphinium nervously.

'Zombie's make honey and other bees sting!' shouted Jason, and then roared with laughter. The Mangold and Delphinium stared at Jason in amazement. He stopped laughing, and gave a deep sigh.

'It was a Knock! Knock! joke!' he explained. 'You're supposed to laugh. I'm a library with a special joke section. But, of course, no one on Space Station Vulnik is allowed to tell jokes. Shall I tell you another one?'

'Don't bother,' said Delphinium. 'I'll just think about that one for a while.'

'Well, out here in this skip-ship I can tell as many jokes as I like,' said Jason defiantly, 'so I'm going to tell one every now and then, even if nobody else knows how to laugh at them.' Then he muttered to Delphinium, 'At least I've put the Mangold off telling his life story.'

14

No Turning Back

Thanks to Delphinium's superb programming, *Dragonfly* skipped merrily through the silver milk of hyperspace until the time came to jump back into ordinary space. The shudder came, and there they were, back in the real world again. As there is no up, down or sideways in ordinary outer space the castle appeared to be the right way up. And Delphinium, Jason and the Mangold could see it was painted in stripes of many different colours ... green, gold, purple, pink and blue ... so that it looked *lively* even though there was no sign of actual *life* about it.

'It's not really a castle, after all,' said Jason. 'It's more like a – a sort of two-storey tent revolving on its own.'

'Well, whatever it is, it's got rings around it

like the planet Saturn,' Delphinium cried. 'One ring, anyway.'

She was right. A strange, wide, flat ring was spinning around the castle, held by the castle's gravity field.

'Forget that ring,' cried the Mangold. 'I'm the pilot of this skip-ship, and now the instrument panel is unjammed, Delphinium can calculate us all the way back to Space Station Vulnik, and I'll be reunited with my dear broom-machines.'

Yet only a bare moment later, a hoarse cry came bursting out from under his two noses.

'Thundersplacket! The instruments are un-jammed, but we still can't turn round,' he yelled. 'We're in the power of a clamp beam. That castle is reeling us in, just as if it had caught us on a hook.'

'That *tent*!' Jason corrected him. 'I'm sure it's what they used to call a big top!'

'Whatever it is, we can't break away from it,' moaned the Mangold. 'Oh, what a ghastly situation for a coward! We're going to plough straight through that cursed ring, being pain-fully injured every five minutes, and then crash into the castle and be utterly killed. And then who's going to oil my broom-machines and comb the fluff out of their bristles, and grease their grungers?'

'I'm too young to die,' moaned Jason. 'I'm only eleven.'

'Well, what about me? Ten for the rest of my life, and the whole rest of my life is only going to last about another ten minutes,' groaned Del-phinium, almost wishing she were nine again.

A few feathers fluttered around them.

'I always moult when I'm frightened,' jab-bered the Mangold.

But, suddenly, Delphinium noticed something unusual, and found she couldn't help being interested, even if she was well into what might be her last ten minutes.

'There are *words* bobbling about in that ring,' she said. 'Look over there!'

'P-O-P . . . Popcorn!' read Jason slowly.

'It's warning us that we will be popped into pieces as small as grains of corn,' howled the Mangold, anxious to keep everyone as terrified as he was, so that his own cowardice did not show up quite as much. 'Ahhhrrr! Here we go!'

With these words, he flung himself flat on the floor, went rigid with panic, drummed with his fists, and waited for the end.

15

Popcorn, Candyfloss and Hot Dogs

There was no crash. The ring seemed to melt away around *Dragonfly*, which shot through it as if through mere cobwebs.

'What sort of ring *is* this?' Delphinium asked, opening her eyes again. 'Can we activate a grab and bring in a sample?'

Between them, she and Jason prized the rigid Mangold off the floor, lightly tapping his joints with a spanner in order to make him bendable once more. The treatment worked: a few taps, and he was as lively as a cricket. They were able to ease him back into the pilot's seat. Doing their best to calm him, they fed him the last crambo bar from the ship's emergency rations – one which Delphinium would dearly have liked for herself for she hadn't had a thing since breakfast, and ranting, raving and roaring, followed by accidents (or adventures) and the telling of life stories, had left her extremely hungry. But the Mangold wolfed it down. Then he activated one of the skip-ship grabs. A thin, jointed arm, with magnetic teeth on the end of it, extended from the nose of *Dragonfly*, snapped up a sample of the ring material, then folded back into the skip-ship control cabin.

'A plastic bag!' exclaimed Delphinium. 'An empty, plastic bag with that strange word *Popcorn* printed on it.'

'And a crinkled-up paper with the mystic inscription, *Candyfloss*,' cried Jason. 'Look! The wrappers of about twenty crambo bars, and a screwed-up paper covered in red smudges!' He smoothed out the red, smudged paper.

'Hot dog!' he read slowly.

The Mangold screamed. 'Look! Look! Spitzenspangleblatt! It's stained with the blood of a poor overheated canine!' Tears of terror immediately ran down on either side of his two noses, and between them, too.

'I'm not so sure,' said Delphinium, staring at the red stuff spread over the bag. Then, daringly, she tasted a tiny morsel at the edge of the stain, closing her eyes as she skilfully analysed it.

'Chilies, ginger, tomato, sugar, vinegar, salt, garlic, onion, modified starch ... oh, and a little caramel to give colour. It's a delicious tomato-and-chili sauce.'

More popcorn bags, Mango-Tango cans, hot dog and candyfloss papers, and the wrappers from crambo bars bounced away on either side of them. The big top (if big top is what it really was) now towered over them. Flags on its towers trembled as photons of light from distant suns struck them. Stretching over everything, including the big top, was the even bigger top of the stars. The Mangold stopped being rigid with fear and went utterly limp – which was just as bad.

'I am prepared for the worst,' he muttered. 'That's probably the airlock door ... that round, black door there. But who's going to open it for us?' He sighed listlessly.

The round, black, airlock door reminded Delphinium of her screen on Space Station Vulnik. It was made of some shiny metal, and dimly reflected the stars of the universe, though of course it reflected them backwards. And now they were rushing furiously at their own reflection with the ghostly reflections of the stars behind.

On either side of the door stood two smiling metal figures in painted, peeling robes. Suddenly, they moved jerkily, swinging to face *Dragonfly*, raising trumpets to their long, curling lips. There is no sound in outer space, but Delphinium imagined the fanfare of the trumpets going out between the stars as a pure wave. And as she imagined this, the door moved, slid open, and they shot through it. As they did so, Delphinium saw a glittering sign flashing on and off in a curious, quavering fashion. She even managed to read it as they sped past. *Free parking*, it said.

'What is this place?' she cried in despair.

Then all the stars vanished, and utter darkness closed in around them.

Part Two

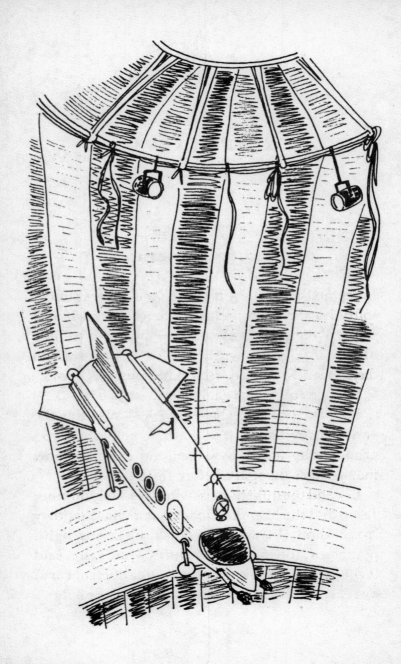

16

A Human Skyscraper

It seemed as if giant hands immediately closed, softly but firmly, on either side of *Dragonfly* and shelved the gallant skip-ship – just as a nimble librarian might have shelved a book in the old days when there had been such things as books.

Silence enveloped them.

Had they been shelved for ever? Was this the end of their story? It is hard to tell when you are actually inside the story and can't see how many pages there are before the end.

Beyond the quartz-glass windows, Delphinium, Jason and the Mangold made out a vast, shadowy space, dimly lit with a reddish, flickering light. Somehow, the big top (for that's what Jason said it was, and you have to believe a qualified library) appeared even bigger inside than outside.

'Well, we can't just stand around doing nothing,' said Delphinium at last.

'Yes, we can! Doing nothing's the easy part,' said Jason. 'Let's tell jokes. For instance, why do idiots eat biscuits?'

'I don't know. Why do idiots eat biscuits?' asked Delphinium rather crossly.

'Because they're crackers,' cried Jason. 'Crackers! Do you get it? Boom! Boom!' Lightning crackled in the air around them, but Jason chuckled to himself, as he turned to look out of the window on the other side of the control cabin.

'Doom! Doom!' quavered the Mangold. 'There's a lot of doom flickering around down there.'

'It's not doom, it's only lightning! Oh, and a bonfire,' Jason shouted. 'I can see it through this window. There's a black shape down there, sitting at a packing-case desk, looking at a computer screen. And down below us there are a lot of other black shapes – different shapes – all holding up burning sticks in the air. Candles, I suppose! I've heard about candles on old story tapes.'

But he was interrupted by an alarming voice which boomed out through the ship-to-spaceport intercom.

'Come on out with your hands up, or you

will all be discombobulated by the overwhelming orders of La Mollerina the magnificent Williwaw of the West.' The Mangold wailed at the mere mention of discombobulation.

'They can't discombobulate us up here,' declared Jason, comforting him. 'They haven't got a ladder.' Yet, even as he spoke, ten of the black shadows, showing amazing skill and balance, leaped on to one another's shoulders to form a human skyscraper. A fierce, whiskery face peered through the quartz glass at them.

'Come on out now, hands above your heads, trembling and begging for mercy as you come,' cried the intercom voice. 'These are the orders of La Mollerina, who also happens to be the woman I adore and the one who adores me back. She is planning to roast you over our campfire, but if you beg and tremble hard enough she might let you off with a mere, light singeing.'

'Crashnabbersnuk!' mumbled the Mangold. 'What did I tell you? Doom! This just proves that cowards often understand what's going on far, far better than brave people. That's why they're cowards in the first place.'

'Come *out*, and come *down*, before we come *up*,' yelled the intercom voice. 'Don't think we're frightened of heights. We are acrobatical pirates and, besides, we're under the magnificent protection of my fiancée, La Mollerina, the Williwaw of the West!'

'I'm already sick of La Mollerina, the Williwaw of the West!' grumbled Jason. 'And we haven't even been introduced.'

'La Mollerina! That name reminds me of something,' said Delphinium, frowning. 'Not the Williwaw part of it, though! What *is* a Williwaw, anyway?'

'A sort of wild wind,' Jason replied. 'And there are no wild winds in outer space.'

'Stop defiling the name of La Mollerina, the Williwaw of the West, with your chitter-chatter!' cried the voice. 'Get down here at once.'

Delphinium looked at Jason.

'At least a scary life is more fun than a boring one,' she said boldly.

Then she opened the skip-ship door.

17

A Wobbly Ladder

When Delphinium and Jason shuffled out of *Dragonfly*, hands over their heads and trembling so magnificently you'd have sworn they'd been practising for years, they found themselves nose to nose with the face on top of the human skyscraper. The skyscraper immediately collapsed backwards. Ten black shadows curved away through the flickering air, somersaulting elegantly in all directions.

She and Jason were left, huddled together outside *Dragonfly*, on a small step about fifty feet above the ground. There were no stairs down. The flickering, sniggering faces looking up at them were mostly humanoid, though a few were rather dragonish, and at least one had a beak. By the flickering of the firelight, Delphinium could see that every shape beneath every face was dressed in close-fitting coloured tights. Catching sight of her, the shapes danced wildly, shouting, 'Prisoners! Real prisoners! We're in business at last. About time, too!' Then they fired ray guns over and over again, and snapped on laser-light swords, filling the air with coloured slashes and streaks.

'Come down, you swabs!' yelled the intercom voice. It came from the middle of what looked like a gorse bush ... a face full of the fiercest whiskers in the whole gang. 'Let's have a look at you!'

'Women and children first,' said the Mangold, trying to crouch down behind Delphinium and Jason.

'How *can* we come down?' called Delphinium crossly. 'There are no stairs, and we can't fly.'

'Form a ladder on the double, you swabs!' ordered the face behind the gorse bush, and some of the figures below tossed their candles and ray guns to others, then flung themselves together in such a way that they actually formed a living ladder stretching right up to Delphinium's space-boots. 'Pirate rigging for anyone who is too scared to jump,' the gorse-bush face called mockingly.

'Don't wave your candles around like that,' Delphinium ordered. 'It makes it hard to see.'

The face behind the gorse bush swelled with fury. 'Candles? These aren't candles! Don't you know a flaming torch when you see one?'

'Well, just be careful with them, whatever they are,' Delphinium answered.

Then, gingerly, she began to scramble down the ladder, which continually wobbled and sagged and complained in various whining voices about how heavy she was, and the way she was digging the toes of her space-boots into the ladder. No sooner had she reached the ground than rough hands seized her. One of the strange crew held a flaming torch so close to her face that she imagined her eyebrows might be singed off.

18

A Problem with Scuppers

'A bratling! A mere, female bratling,' cried the voice from the gorse-bush face, which she could now see was a young face in spite of the whiskers. She looked past the face and, over by the bonfire, she could make out someone sitting beside a ramshackle box on which was a small computer.

'I didn't know pirates had computers?' she cried suspiciously.

'Being a pirate is nothing but a part-time, temporary job for me,' said the woman, sitting beside the box. She had a husky voice which sounded extremely pleased with itself. 'Soon, I shall be moving on to other, much grander things.' This person could be none other than La Mollerina herself.

'She's going to be Queen of the Universe

almost immediately,' cried the gorse-bush face, 'which means I'm going to be King of the Universe, ha! ha! ha! King of the whole caboodle – for she loves me passionately. Me, Bamba Caramba, the scourge of outer space. Bamba Caramba is *me*,' he added, slapping his own chest, in case they were in any doubt about it, 'and these galleygangers are our crew of piratical space dogs!' Then a lot of other voices began laughing in a very wicked way.

'Ay, ay, Captain!'

'Right you are, me hearties!' he replied.

'Shall we fling them into the scuppers, Captain?'

'What are scuppers?' asked Delphinium nervously. Whatever they were, they sounded wet and slippery.

'The scuppers were openings in the sides of ancient sea-going ships,' said Jason from behind her, 'so that sea water could run off the deck. Libraries know things like that. And I also know you don't have scuppers on a space ship.'

'Forget the scuppers,' said La Mollerina. 'We've got a plank – that one, leaning against the wall over there. Make them walk it.'

There was another silence, a rather shocked one this time.

'But if they walk the plank,' said a pirate with smeary glasses, 'won't they fall into the utterly empty, airless, eternal void of outer space?'

'So what?' said La Mollerina, who was obviously utterly ruthless – the worst kind of space pirate. Rising gracefully to her feet, she strolled towards them, then put her elbow on Bamba Caramba's head (for he was not particularly tall) and leaned casually on him, as a librarian might lean on the desk where books are issued.

From where she was standing, Delphinium, looking past Bamba Caramba and La Mollerina, could see the screen of the computer. Numbers were counting down . . . 10,002, 10,001, 10,000. Something was about to happen, but what? And when?

'My dearest little Williwaw,' said Bamba Caramba in a troubled voice, rolling his eyes upward as he spoke. 'My darling, wicked one, of course I passionately adore your sinful schemes, but do hang on a moment! If they walk the plank into the empty, airless, eternal void of space where there is no air pressure, they will immediately swell up and explode.'

'All the better!' shouted La Mollerina. 'A dictionary, indeed! Once I'm Queen of the Universe I'll change the meaning of a whole lot of words. For instance "magnificent" and "marvellous" will only be allowed to apply to *me*, La Mollerina. They go together – like strawbarrels and chrome.'

'You mean strawberries and cream,' said Jason. La Mollerina gritted her teeth as she glanced at him.

'See what I mean?' she asked the pirates. 'That's the sort of know-it-all attitude you get from libraries. Do we want that sort of thing going on around us?'

'Shame! Shame!' yelled all the pirates.

'Anyone upsetting me with corrections will walk the plank,' cried La Mollerina. 'That means getting rid of every, single know-it-all library. So we might as well make this pair walk the plank right now. It'll be more merciful in the long run. And, by the way, Bamba, when you speak to me in public, call me "Your Majesty".'

'But we're engaged,' said Bamba Caramba. 'Calling you "Your Majesty" doesn't sound very loving.'

'Call me "Your Majesty" until the rapturous day of our wedding,' said La Mollerina, sounding rather bored by the thought of the rapturous day. She strolled back to the computer, and carefully switched it off. 'We must save the batteries until full power is restored.'

'Bow!' shouted Bamba Caramba, flapping an arm at Delphinium and Jason. 'Bow when the magnificent Williwaw walks by.' Though Jason and Delphinium bowed deeply, they put their

hands behind their backs and kept their fingers crossed.

'Down with all libraries!' said La Mollerina, glancing at her watch. 'The plank for both of them! Down with all histories, encyclopedias, and dictionaries, too!'

'Actually, there's no up or down in space . . . ' Jason began, but Delphinium hastily interrupted him before he made things worse with his corrections.

'I'm not a library. I'm a calculator,' she explained, straightening up because she couldn't go on bowing to someone who was about to make her walk the plank.

'Oh, I'm going to get shot of all calculators, too,' said La Mollerina. 'I'm not having any nonsense from numbers. When I'm queen, numbers are going to add up to whatever I tell them to. That's what being Queen of the Universe means − telling everybody what everything else has to add up to.'

La Mollerina was about six feet tall. She wore pirate-queen clothes, and an eyepatch with a small hole in the middle of it so that she could look through it. But the most remarkable thing about her was her blue hair which stuck out in all directions like bolts of electricity, and which was thick with hair gel. She gave Delphinium and Jason a disdainful look.

'It's the plank for both of you!' she sneered.

But, at that moment, shrill screams of the sort pirates often give when they are alarmed broke out overhead. The whole ladder collapsed into a groaning, moaning heap. At once something like an earthquake began in the middle of the heap.

'And what have we here?' Bamba cried, twirling his rusty sword. But even he fell silent as the Mangold slowly rose to his full height, brushing various pirates, all of whom were weedy (though wiry as well), from his shoulders as he did so.

NEW
BROOMS
SWEEP
CLEAN

19

Love and Television

A dead silence fell. The Mangold certainly
looked impressive. Being so tall, his face reached
up out of the firelight into the shadows, and in
the poor light his expression of terror was easily
mistaken for one of reckless courage. All that
the pirates (including La Mollerina herself)
could really see was someone who was seven-
feet tall, muscular – from sweeping and dusting
for an entire ten-level space station – someone
dressed in pink tights and vest similar to their
own, and wearing a large medal pinned to his
chest. What they could *not* see was that this
medal was merely a badge awarded for twenty
years of dedicated sweeping and dusting, and
not for grappling with ferocious aliens on the
frontiers of space. The Mangold glanced around
desperately.

'This place needs a thorough going-over,' he began. He meant that it needed to be tidied up, and that he would offer to tidy it up himself for very low wages, or even for nothing. The pirates, however, thought he was offering to attack them all at once.

'Gadzooks!' cried La Mollerina. '*This* is something like a man.'

It was hard to tell in the uncertain light, but her expression had changed. She seemed to be looking at the Mangold with deep admiration. Delphinium wondered whether to tell her that the Mangold, though something *like* a man, was really something else.

'Two noses!' La Mollerina cried in delight. 'You know, I've often thought that having just one was a bad mistake. I mean why have one of anything if you can have two, instead?'

The pirates all began nodding hard, agreeing with La Mollerina. 'Fancy one man – *one man* – threatening to give the whole thirty-seven of us a thorough going-over!' they muttered to each other.

'He's a shade too tall, but apart from that, he's perfect,' said La Mollerina. She glanced at her watch as if, for some reason, she was anxious to keep track of the time. 'We'll give him a choice.' She looked deeply into the Mangold's eyes. 'Do you want to join our crew?'

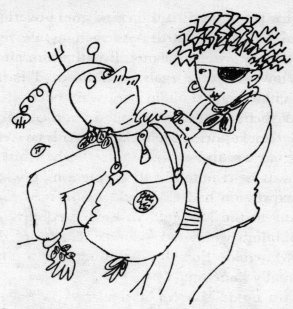

'Or would you prefer to be hung upside down for a week and then flung into the scuppers ... ' began Bamba Caramba. The Mangold gave a roar. Delphinium and Jason knew at once it was a roar of terror, but Bamba took it for a roar of rage. 'Gently flung! *Gently* flung, of course!' he yelled quickly. 'Playfully flung, really!' But the next moment he was flung himself, and not too playfully at that. La Mollerina hoisted him up by his collar, and then tossed him scornfully aside.

'Silence!' she commanded. 'The more closely I look at this fellow, the more certain I am that he is the one for me. He's a shade *too* tall, but he can stand well back behind me, and that'll make him look shorter. As soon as we reach some fairly civilized planet, I shall marry him.'

'You said you'd marry *me*!' shouted Bamba Caramba.

'Well, I've changed my mind,' said La Mollerina. 'I'm suddenly seeing things with new eyes. *Pooh* to shortness and gorse-bush whiskers! Hoorah for two noses and purple eyes, is what I say now!'

The Mangold stood quavering, torn between loyalty to friends, supreme terror at the thought of plank-walking, and ordinary terror at the prospect of sudden marriage.

'It's a tempting offer,' he muttered at last, 'but I can't betray my companions. No! Never! Not to be thought of.'

'Oh, yeah! yeah! Very noble! Such noble instincts do you credit,' said La Mollerina sounding as if she were anxious to get this part of the conversation over and done with as quickly as possible. 'But my word is law. It's either that, or walk the plank and explode in the empty, airless, eternal void of space. No choice, really.'

'Put like that I might change my mind,' mumbled the Mangold.

'You must learn to sound much more affectionate,' La Mollerina said, giving him a sharp jab with her elbow. 'I'll forgive you this once. But from now on, whenever I speak, you must stare lovingly into my eyes. If you crouch a bit you'll be able to look straight into them.'

Broom-masters don't get much practice at staring lovingly into anyone's eyes, but the Mangold did well for a beginner.

'Not bad!' said La Mollerina. 'Not great, but not bad, either. Now, let's become better acquainted over a firkin of Mango-Tango and a few glop sandwiches.' She glanced at her watch again. 'Perhaps we could watch a little television. That often brings people together.'

At the mention of television, the Mangold's loving glance became ten times as affectionate as it had been before. Bamba Caramba glowered sulkily.

'The power system here is temporarily out of action,' La Mollerina went on. 'That's why we have to make do with flaming torches. However, there *is* a battery-powered wall-sized television screen in the ticket office,' she said enticingly. 'We were just about to watch episode one million of *Intergalactic Hospital*, and follow it up with episode one million-and-one.'

The Mangold began a frenzied mumbling and double-nosed snuffling. Suddenly, he seemed not only cowardly, but highly unreliable as well.

'After all, I haven't known these kids very long,' Delphinium heard him muttering. 'I expect marriage is quite pleasant provided you do what you're told. And, after all, every man has his price.' Then he flung his arms wide, and cried to La Mollerina, 'Take me! I'm yours.'

Some of the pirates applauded. Others glanced nervously at Bamba Caramba who was looking extremely displeased.

'You're not getting your ring back,' he yelled. 'It stays on my finger!'

'I'll get it back when I want to,' hissed La Mollerina, looking highly wicked. 'You won't miss a finger, or possibly two.'

But Delphinium was nudging Jason.

'They've forgotten us,' she whispered. 'They're not watching us at all. Let's run for it!'

'Do you think we can?' asked Jason. 'I mean – I know about walking and even prancing, but running . . . ' Even as he spoke, however, he found himself running most efficiently. Off they sped, using a special tip-toe running, exactly right for a situation like this. It seemed to come quite naturally.

Overhead, the ceiling rustled with strings of silken flags and banners, stretching criss-cross in every direction. To their left, Delphinium saw a door with a glass shutter set in it, and the words *Ticket Office* printed across it in large letters. Beyond the ticket office, she caught a glimpse of *Dragonfly*, settled snugly in a parking slot, but looking curiously defenceless and small. There, in the slot beside *Dragonfly*, was something that looked like a stone shed, painted black with a skull-and-cross-bones on it, and, beyond that, there were not just dozens but hundreds of skip-ship slots, all empty.

Delphinium suddenly understood just where they were and what they were in (apart from serious trouble, that is).

'Jason! This great, big space is nothing but a parking lot,' she cried aloud. 'But who'd need room to park hundreds of skip-ships all at the same time? And why?'

20

Across the Parking Lot

The pirates heard her.

'Get them! Get them!' they shouted.

There was an immediate thunder of feet, hooves, claws and wooden legs.

'Har! Har! Har! We are the bloodthirsty, death-defying, dirty-dog-darstards of the parking lot,' the pirates cried, setting off after Jason and Delphinium. 'Har! Har! We *stole* this parking lot! It's ours now!'

Delphinium and Jason raced past a series of dark purple doors, all of which seemed to be jammed open with remarkable objects . . . a big red-and-white striped beach ball, a small, stuffed dinosaur, a magnifying glass, a hamburger made of sponge rubber, strings of rubber sausages, and a lot of false pies. They both realized that, before they could get the elevator

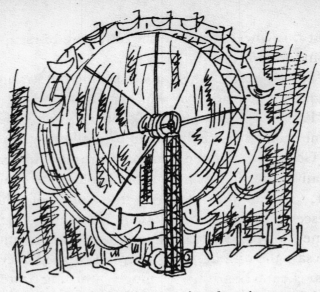

doors free and working again, the pirates would have caught up with them, so they ran desperately past the elevators, hoping to find another way of escape from the parking lot.

And there, almost beyond the light of the bonfire, Delphinium thought, for a moment, that she saw a great arm beckoning them on. She looked again.

It was a huge spinning wheel with little crescent-shaped chairs dangling down from it. The wheel carried these crescent-shaped chairs up out of the firelight, into the shadows just under the ceiling, back down again into the firelight, and then up into the shadows once more. It made Delphinium's stomach feel peculiar just looking at it, but she knew, at once, that this wheel might be the only way to escape from the pirates.

'Faster! Faster!' she panted, feeling the strangest pain in her side just over her ribs.

'Faster! Faster!' panted Jason at exactly the same moment. 'We'll have to be really quick!'

'Got her!' shouted Bamba Caramba triumphantly. But just as he put out his hand to grab her, Delphinium leaped into one of the crescent-shaped carriages. A moment later, something thumped down on top of her, and she saw the dim light of Jason's illustrated overalls. The wheel was turning – turning faster and faster, sweeping them up and away.

Jason and Delphinium untangled themselves. One of the pirates had leaped in between the carriages and had somehow made the motor speed up. Down whizzed Delphinium and Jason, then up they whistled, and over they wheeled. Across the parking lot, by the flickering light of the bonfire, Delphinium could see La Mollerina and the Mangold still practising loving glances.

'Well, they won't get off *that* wheel in a hurry. Look at the way it's whizzing round!' shouted Bamba Caramba. 'Har har har! But let's bounce back before that lanky, loblolly steals the heart of my magnificent Williwaw. If there's any stealing around here, it's going to be us that's doing it. Come on, lads: back to the ticket office! Glop sandwiches and television, lads! And *then*, by golly, we'll make them walk the plank.'

'Arrr! Arrr!' cried the pirates full of enthusiasm, as they made off into the firelight, har-har-harring, and carrying the torches with them. Delphinium imagined them all settling down in front of the television (something she had never been allowed to watch), munching glop sandwiches as they revelled in *Intergalactic Hospital*. What luxury! On the other hand, their pirate queen seemed to be a woman who could turn particularly nasty. In some ways it felt better to be whizzing round and round on a big wheel than trying to please La Mollerina, the Williwaw of the West.

'Oh dear,' she sighed. 'I've come through hyperspace, halfway around the edge of the known universe. I've told my life story, climbed down a living ladder, and run away from space pirates. Now, I'm going round and round on this big wheel, and I still haven't had a single thing to eat since breakfast. I'm starving.'

'Me too!' said Jason.

21

On the Ferris Wheel

'It's all that Mangold's fault!' Delphinium cried in fury. 'He ate the last crambo bar.'

'Well, remember, he *is* a coward,' said Jason. 'Shaking in his shoes must give him a good appetite.'

'There are some things that even cowardice cannot excuse,' said Delphinium. 'What will we do now?'

'I don't know about you, but I'm going to tell a joke . . . a bird joke,' cried Jason. 'That's what you do in times of danger to keep your spirits up. Are you ready? Listen closely! Did you hear of the farmer who put corn in his gumboots because he was pigeon-toed?'

There was a sudden flash of lightning. Jason glanced around anxiously, but, in spite of being so hungry, Delphinium suddenly caught a glimpse of just what a joke might mean. 'Oh, I see,' she exclaimed. 'Words going in two directions at once!' And somehow, being a prisoner on a ferris wheel, longing for a crambo bar, and listening to a library telling a joke, seemed such a silly situation to be in that a strange butterfly (well, it certainly felt like a butterfly) began turning flips somewhere inside her. Then a whole flock of butterflies came fluttering up through her throat, and as she opened her mouth to set them free, a new sound came out of her. A laugh . . . not much of a laugh but it was a real laugh for all that – Delphinium's first laugh ever. The lightning flashed yet again.

Delphinium just happened to have tossed her head back so that her struggling new laugh would leap out as freely as possible, and that was how she came to see something that turned the laugh into a gasp of amazement. The faint glow of Jason's fluorescent illustrations lit up the ceiling as they swept under it, and there in the ceiling, directly overhead, was a strange, round patch of darkness that was even darker-than-dark. It was an open trapdoor.

'How can things suddenly become so peculiar?' Jason was saying. 'It seems only a moment ago that you were calculating, and I was prancing around on Space Station Vulnik, doing a bit of useful library work. As for the Mangold – he was sweeping level four, and all of us were as happy as squeedles in summer. Now, here we are, you and me, sitting on a ferris wheel . . . for that's what we're on, if you want to know! A ferris wheel! And the Mangold is suddenly engaged to marry a pirate queen.'

'Forget all that!' Delphinium cried. 'Didn't you see it?'

'See what?' asked Jason.

'A way out, or rather *up*! A trapdoor in the ceiling.'

By now, they were sweeping up towards the ceiling, and were almost under the trapdoor once more.

Leaping up in her seat, which wobbled alarmingly, Delphinium quickly made the most important calculation of her life. Adding a wild wobble-factor to her calculations, she bent her knees, and jumped. For a dread fraction of a fearful second she seemed to hang helplessly among the shadows. Then her fingers closed on the edge of the trapdoor and hung on tightly.

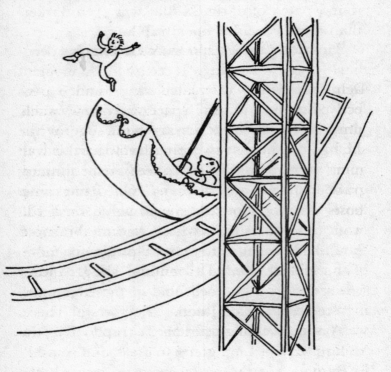

22

Into the Darker-than-Dark

Delphinium had calculated the distance perfectly. She had worked out exactly how much jump-power she needed to reach the edge. What she hadn't worked out was just how hard it was going to be to hold on to that edge once she had grabbed it. Her fingers slipped. One hand came loose. 'I'm going to fall,' she thought. 'First, I'll crash, and then I'll smash.' It was the most terrifying moment of her life. 'This is much more of an accident than an adventure,' she groaned.

But then she grabbed hold of the edge once more, and as she did this . . . hey presto! There was Jason, dangling beside her.

'Help! Help! I am going to crash and smash!' he cried.

'Be brave!' yelled Delphinium. 'Hold on tightly.'

'I am!' said Jason. 'Terribly tightly.'

'Let's say, one-two-three and pull hard,' Delphinium ordered. 'One-two-three!' Slowly she struggled, until she had hooked one foot over the edge of the trapdoor space. Then she took a breath, pulled with her fingers, pushed with her foot (while the other foot waved wildly over the void beneath) and wriggled her elbows over the trapdoor edge. After that it seemed almost easy. Delphinium hauled herself up, rolled into the darker-than-dark, and lay there, panting.

'Are you there, Delphinium?' called Jason's voice, and she saw the glow of his illustrated clothes. He had pulled himself safely into the darker-than-dark beside her.

'It *is* dark, isn't it?' he murmured. 'And spooky!'

'Never mind,' Delphinium cried. 'Remember, this isn't just an accident . . . it's an adventure, too. Let's *pretend* it's fun.'

As she said this something seemed to happen around them. The blackness grew grainy as if it had suddenly cracked all over, letting light come through from somewhere behind it. Then it closed up, and settled down again. But after it had settled down again the blackness was not quite the same blackness it had been. Somehow it was a slightly *lighter* shade of black, although it was still much too dark to see.

'Get away from the trapdoor before we fall through it again,' she cried, 'and let's see if we can't find a wall somewhere. There must be something behind all this darker-than-dark.'

'Did you hear of the butcher who backed into the mincer and got a little behind in his work?' whispered Jason, trying to cheer himself up with one of his own jokes.

The darkness quivered again. And when that infinitesimal quivering stopped, there was no doubt about it: the darkness had stopped being a light sort of darkness and had become a dark sort of lightness.

'I think I can actually see you,' said Jason. 'And look at that weird light. Where is it coming from?'

It was true. A strange, greasy, green glow was oozing around the floor like spilled glue. It seemed to be pushing its way from under a small door.

'Through here!' said Delphinium bravely. 'After all, we have to go somewhere.' She twisted the handle and pulled the little door open. The horrible, green light swept out to meet her. But, though Delphinium was alarmed by this menacing glow, something else was puzzling her even more.

'Jason, why did it suddenly grow lighter a moment ago?' she asked.

'I don't know, but it's happened twice now,' he replied. 'More than twice! Remember those flashes of lightning we saw from the ferris wheel? Delphinium, where are we? What is this place? What is a *ticket office*? Why does it need a car park or a ferris wheel? What *is* this green glow? What's going on?'

'We'll probably find out soon,' Delphinium said. 'We've been totally brave so far. A bit more courage probably won't do us any harm.' But then Jason gave a gasp of horror.

'Look! Look!' he gasped. 'Giant hedgehogs.'

Sure enough, there in front of them, illuminated by the green glow, were three horrible, huge, spiky shapes, arms raised in a threatening fashion.

'What are hedgehogs?' Delphinium whispered, for they had no such things on Space Station Vulnik.

'They're insectivorous quadrupeds,' said Jason.

'Whisper, or they might hear us and charge forward and crush us under their wheels,' said Delphinium.

'What? Wheels? Hang on a moment!' Jason cried. 'Hedgehogs don't have wheels.'

Delphinium looked more closely. She relaxed and laughed. Now she'd learned how to do it, laughing was surprisingly easy.

'They're *broom-machines*,' she said. 'Jason, we're in a broom cupboard.'

Jason groaned.

'Do you mean we've travelled through space, escaped from a lot of bloodthirsty pirates by ferris wheel, been whisked up into the darker-than-dark, then tumbled into a greasy, green glow only to find ourselves in a broom cupboard?' he cried incredulously. 'Where's this green glow coming from, anyway?' Then his voice changed abruptly. 'Ugh! What's *that*!'

Jason and Delphinium both stared upwards in horror. A horrible, slimy, green something hung from the ceiling, dangling and dripping as if it had been dead for days and days.

'I hate the look of it, whatever it is,' whispered Delphinium uneasily.

'Ugh! Double ugh! Urrrrgh! Yeecchch! And there's more than one of them,' said Jason. He could make out a second green shape hanging in slimy stillness beside the first, and then a third, a fourth and a fifth. Indeed, the ceiling was covered with slimy, green danglers.

'They look like . . . like chrysalises,' said Delphinium doubtfully.

'I don't want to see any butterfly that comes

out of chrysalises like those,' Jason said. 'They'd be dreadful blood-sucking butterflies with long fangs.'

'Or vampire bats,' suggested Delphinium, with a shudder.

'Vampire boots!' said Jason. 'Vampire boots with blood on their tongues. Ha! That's funny!' And he laughed at the thought of vampire boots.

The dark-lightness cracked and grew lighter. But neither of them really noticed it this time for, as if they had somehow managed to swallow Jason's laughter, the chrysalises swelled and seethed and writhed in a loathsome fashion.

'Look! Across there!' Delphinium cried with relief. 'Another door! One in, one out! Let's go!'

For some mysterious reason, of all the accidents of the last hour or two, sharing the broom cupboard with those slimy chrysalises was by far the worst.

23

The Great Ring

Where had the moving-carpet of the story – the ins, outs, bumps and jumps of the tale – carried Jason and Delphinium by now? They looked around and found that they were standing on the edge of a huge and shadowy ring, surrounded by hundreds of empty seats. And from the shadows, all around the ring, came a fearsome, growling sound, as if a fleet of space ships (with broken grungers) was trying to take off from a high-gravity planet.

Most people would have fallen to the ground, stricken with panic by this terrible growling coming out of deep, dark shadows. But Delphinium and Jason jammed fingers into their ears, and bravely edged forward. All around them they felt the presence of a thousand ghostly listeners. Somehow, the great ring felt invisibly crowded with cheering, clapping people, waving hats and eating crambo bars. Yet every seat was empty.

'We've left pirates and hedgehogs behind us. Now, we've come to the kingdom of one-eyed frogs,' said Jason, pointing at a curious, squatting shape with a single, glassy eye.

'It's a spotlight,' Delphinium exclaimed. 'Look! There are lots of them!' She held out a hand towards the spotlight, and it lit up, giving off a curiously weary, reluctant light. Both Delphinium and Jason looked fearfully along its dull, yellow beam. There were no chrysalises dangling overhead, and no flags and banners, either. Instead, the upper air was crisscrossed with ropes and strings, as if space had started coming apart and someone had tried tying it all together again, using complicated knots. And there, high above them, were seven people in silver tights, hanging by their knees from silver bars, held by silver ropes, and every one of them apparently sound asleep in mid-air.

'But how can anyone sleep hanging upside down?' wondered Delphinium admiringly.

'Bats do it all the time,' said Jason. 'Anyway, look! There's a net under them in case they fall.'

'Still, it's a funny place to sleep,' Delphinium said, twiddling another spotlight into life. 'Oh look! Over there! A whole pile of people! But what's happened to them all? Why are they lying around like that?'

For, as their eyes became used to the half light, Delphinium and Jason could see the big ring was littered with people flopped down all anyhow, and very strange people some of them were!

'They're all *snoring*!' said Jason uneasily. 'What planet do you think this lot comes from?'

He was looking at a whole pile of brightly-coloured men and women, lying crisscross like the lines in a game of multidimensional noughts and crosses. Though they were dressed in rags, tags, socks, frocks, frills and furbelows, every single one of them had a round, red nose held on with elastic. And on either side of these red noses, their eyes were tightly closed. Two of them had somehow crawled free from the rest and were sitting, propped up against one another, back to back. Jason and Delphinium studied these two closely. The first one was bald, except for tufts of blue hair standing out around ears as big as dinner plates, while the other, who had green curls rippling around a white face with bright, red cheeks, wore a frilly dress and a pointed hat that looked exactly like an ice-cream cone jammed upside down on her curls. They both must have been dreaming wonderfully happy dreams though, for huge smiles curled around under their red noses, filling up most of their faces. Caught between the man's limp fingers was a big hoop, covered with dark blue silky paper on which was printed a laughing, golden sun, winking one eye at them.

'They look so happy, it seems a pity to wake them,' said Jason, forgetting to whisper.

Then a curious thing happened. At the sound of his voice, the seven silver people uncrooked their knees, and somersaulted through the air, tumbling into the safety net, where they bounced four times. It was like seeing seven shooting stars suddenly turn flips. But the tumblers didn't wake. They slept on soundly, as if two somersaults, four bounces, and a flip or two were not worth waking for.

But something else caught Jason's eye. Stretched out under the lowest row of seats, snoring like a road drill and dressed in a scarlet loin cloth, lay a huge man, bulging with many more muscles than most people need. He made mere sleeping look like something that only very strong people could do.

'And look over here!' cried Delphinium, moving further on to a gap between two blocks of seats. 'Who are these men and women? What sort of uniform is it they're wearing? And what are those curly things with spouts? Ancient ray guns?'

'No way!' exclaimed Jason scornfully. 'That's a trombone, and that's a tuba! And this one here's a trumpet. Delphinium! This can only be a brass band. I thought brass bands were extinct.'

'Well, they're all asleep, and that's the next best thing,' said Delphinium.

And they prowled in and out of the shadows and between the rows of seats, finding even stranger people, every single one of whom was sound asleep.

24

The Sleeping-beauties

'These people need rescuing from whatever it is that's made them sleep like this,' said Jason, as they came back to the seats they had started out from. 'Anyhow, we just *have* to stop that snoring! Which one shall we rescue first?'

'Let's do the alien with the big ears,' cried Delphinium. For some reason she really liked the look of this big-eared alien and his funny, green-haired partner. 'They look like good fun.' And, by now, she barely noticed how the spot-lights grew a little brighter at the mention of 'fun', or how the shadows stepped back among the empty seats.

'Let's wake them up first, then rescue them afterwards,' Jason said. 'Waking them will be the easy bit.' But waking them wasn't easy at all. In fact, it turned out to be impossible.

They began with gentle shaking, went on to rough shaking and then to the complete earthquake treatment. The man with the big ears, and the woman with the green hair, slept on, smiling to themselves as if they were having delightful dreams. Delphinium shouted, 'Wakey! Wakey!' (an ancient waking spell) in one of the man's huge ears, and Jason told a joke about a dentist, a crocodile and a chocolate cake in the other. Both spotlights grew brighter, but the big-eared man seemed to sink more deeply than ever into sleep.

'I think we have an attack of the sleeping-beauties here,' said Jason at last. 'I thought it was a fairy-tale sickness, but it's turned out to be true. Perhaps they'll only wake when someone kisses them. Not me,' he added hastily. 'Some prince or other.'

'Where are we going to get a prince out here in infinite space?' cried Delphinium.

'*You* kiss them then, and we'll see what happens,' said Jason.

'How *do* you kiss someone?' asked Delphinium. 'You tell me and I'll do it, no matter how dangerous it is.'

'You . . . you sort of press your lips against someone,' said Jason uncertainly. 'I think!' he added. Delphinium stared at him disbelievingly.

'What good does that do?' she asked.

'I don't know,' said Jason. 'But it's in all the stories. It's supposed to be nice.'

'Well, I'll give it a go,' said Delphinium, and pressed her lips against the rim of one of the man's ears. But his eyelids did not so much as flutter.

'*Your* turn,' Delphinium said firmly to Jason. But he made a dreadful fuss about this simple task, saying that kissing green-haired women wasn't part of a library's work, and so on. At last, however, he planted a rather bad-tempered kiss on the ice-cream cone-hat, but the woman did not wake.

'We're obviously doing something wrong!' cried Delphinium. 'You probably have to practise for years to get it one hundred per cent right.'

'I wish I knew what they were grinning about,' said Jason grumpily, for he thought that if he went to all the trouble of kissing someone, then the very least that someone could do was to wake up, smiling, and say thank you.

But at this moment Delphinium found she was looking into a space that had been dark with shadows when they first arrived in the giant circle. Now the shadows had faded, she saw something that made her forget all about kissing and sleeping-beauties.

'A food funnel!' she yelled. 'Jason, it actually *is* a food funnel.' For Delphinium, that food funnel seemed like the most marvellous discovery they had made since being whooshed away by the skip-ship *Dragonfly*.

25

Skudge, Grabfabbit, Chuckleberry Ice-cream and Various Pies

Jason immediately lost interest in all the sleeping-beauties. Delphinium was right. There, in a gap between the seats, set into the wall, was a food funnel, with a catching-tray below it. A menu in all the major galactic languages was pasted on to the wall beside it. Merely reading the menu made Delphinium and Jason feel faint with longing.

'There are seventy different sorts of pie on this menu,' said Jason, frowning. 'Who needs seventy different kinds of pie?'

'I do! I'm starving.' Delphinium sighed. 'I was hungry when I finished roaring, ranting and raving, and now it's ten times worse. Punch in everything at once!'

'Or even sooner,' said Jason, punching away.

'I'm going to have scrummits to start off with, and then a big bowlful of chuckleberry ice-cream.'

'Scrummits!' exclaimed Delphinium, peering at the menu which was flickering on and off in an uncertain way. 'Oh, I want scrummits, too. Punch in *two* helpings of scrummits.'

Jason pressed the menu button with the number 26 on it. There was a whirring sound. A pink light trembled on-off, on-off, in a sickly fashion. They waited, staring at the catching-tray, greedily at first, and then with increasing dismay. Just as it seemed their hopes were coming to nothing, there was a rustle, then a twang, and then a clonking sound. A small bowl slid wearily out of the food funnel on to the catching-tray. But the bowl was greasy, even chipped, and there was only a single, cold, fat-encrusted scrummit lying in the bottom of it.

Quickly, Delphinium snatched up the scrum-mit and, frowning, pressed number 31 – chuckleberry ice-cream. The pink light flashed on-off, on-off. Nothing happened. It flashed again. Then, at last, a small blob of half-melted ice-cream and five chuckleberries, all rather withered and mouldy, appeared on the tray.

And it was while she stood staring at that small, melting spoonful of chuckleberry ice-cream that something clicked in Delphinium's calculator mind. Something suddenly seemed so clear to her, that she couldn't help wondering why it had taken her so long to recognize it (though of course even the best calculators can't help being distracted by scuppers, sound effects, loathsome, writhing chrysalises, aliens with huge ears, and brass bands suffering from the sleeping-beauty illness, not to mention the ancient art of kissing). Yet, in spite of all these distracting adventures, the calculating part of Delphinium's mind had been privately hard at work, and now it suddenly came up with a brilliant idea.

'Jason, tell jokes at once!' she commanded. 'Do it now! Don't waste time asking questions.' She sounded so fierce that Jason did as he was told without arguing.

'Why did Farmer Jones make his chickens swim in hot water?' he asked in a quavering voice.

'I don't know! Why *did* Farmer Jones make his chickens swim in hot water?' asked Delphinium.

'So they would lay hard-boiled eggs! Boom! Boom!' shouted Jason, recovering quickly and laughing at his own joke.

The air brightened. The items on the menu flashed pink and blue. The green light deepened and blinked more strongly, and suddenly a huge bowl of chuckleberry ice-cream tumbled out on to the catching-tray.

'Another joke!' demanded Delphinium.

'What comes out of the forest on sixteen legs?' asked Jason. As he spoke, Delphinium was once more punching in several delicious items from the menu.

'I don't know. What *does* come out of the forest on sixteen legs?' she asked, punching away.

'Snow White and the seven dwarfs. Get it, Delphinium?' cried Jason, and, though Delphinium had never heard of Snow White and the seven dwarfs, she laughed as heartily as she could.

The green light flashed, and suddenly dishes of wonderful food tumbled on to the steel tray. There were at least two dozen scrummits, crambo bars, squares of snigfobblemee, delicately-coloured glasses filled to the brim with sparkling glishy-glugglug, grabfabbit-and-skudge dinners, a whole block of momba swimming in toffee cream sauce, ramekins of Qxixt fruit oysters, and pies of every description.

'It's a feast!' cried Jason. 'How did you do it?'

'*You* did it,' said Delphinium in a modest moment, rare for a grade-A calculator. 'Well, *we* did it,' she added hastily, not wanting him to get too conceited. 'You did it with your jokes, and I did it with my laughing, and we both did it by having fun. Remember how lightning flashed in the parking lot when I laughed for the very first time? Remember how the darker-than-dark grew merely dark when you told a joke just outside the broom cupboard? Eat as much as you can *while* you can. We don't know what is going to happen next.'

'I know my jokes are good,' said Jason, 'but I didn't know they were *that* good. It was really clever of you to make the connection.'

Delphinium looked modest once more.

'I realized that any time we actually began enjoying our accidents we restored fun-energy to the system. There was almost no fun-energy left anywhere. I'd say this place has had a brush with the Acropola.' Her expression changed. 'Listen!'

'What is it?' cried Jason listening.

'Nothing,' said Delphinium. 'Don't you realize that there's suddenly nothing to hear? The snoring's stopped.'

Yet at that moment there was a soft scruffling sound behind them and then a stretching and groaning. Like a chain of mountains lifting out of the first oceans, the huge muscle-man was actually sitting up. A quiver of movement ran all around the great ring. Suddenly, yawning and stretching could be heard on every side.

Over in the net the seven people in silver tights were also stirring. The man with the big ears was on his feet, staggering around in a confused fashion. His green-haired companion winked and blinked but, even when she saw Jason and Delphinium, her smile did not leave her face.

'Where are we?' she asked in a dazed voice.

'We don't know,' said Jason. 'We were hoping *you'd* be able to tell us.'

The green-haired woman looked around.

'We'll begin at the beginning,' she said. 'This is the main ring. I do know that.'

'The main ring?' cried Delphinium. 'The main ring of what?'

The green-haired woman gave her a pitying glance.

'The main ring of the Wonder Show, of course,' she cried. 'What else could it be?'

Part Three

26

The Wonder Show Wakes

'The Wonder Show?' yelled Delphinium. 'Is this really the Wonder Show?'

'Of course it is,' said the man with big ears.

'Well, at last we know *where* we are,' Jason said with a sigh of pleasure.

'Yes, but every "where" is somewhere inside another "where" and I don't know which "where" this "where" happens to be *in* right now,' said the green-haired woman.

'Then it must be very *wearing*,' said Jason, for now he had been praised for making jokes, he found it hard to stop. 'Delphinium, there's a big reward for finding the Wonder Show. But have we found it, or has it found us?'

'Is there a reward for finding *you*?' asked the man with the big ears eagerly. Jason shook his head sadly.

'There ought to be, but there isn't,' he said. 'We're only kids.'

'Then the reward ought to be twice as much,' the woman cried. 'Kids are definitely the most important people in the universe. But how did you come to be here? Were you left behind? Or did you buy a ticket at the ticket office?'

'No,' said Delphinium. 'We were just wondering a while ago what a ticket office was. This is Jason, the famous joke-and-reference library, and I am Delphinium, the much *more* famous calculator from level seven of Space Station Vulnik,' she added rather boastfully. 'And we're both orphans.'

'You interest me strangely,' said the big-eared man, staring at her intently. 'Orphans are usually children who have lost their parents, but we feel (Martha and me, that is) that parents who have lost their children are orphans, too.'

'Yes we *do*,' agreed the green-haired woman. 'Tell me, have we ever met before?' But she was interrupted by the strong man.

'Food! Food!' he roared in a hoarse, impatient voice. 'Food before family tales! Meals before manners! Give me crumpets with jam, or I shall faint. Give me scrummits and gingered quob. Stoke me up on chocolate bars, applecrumpf, sundaes, melon slices, crambo, and scoops of chuckleberry ice-cream with inky fingers.'

'Inky fingers?' cried Delphinium in horror.

'Inky fingers are strips of pancake soaked in blackberry juice and essence of tigerflower,' explained Jason quickly, partly to reassure Delphinium, and partly to remind the strong man what inky fingers really were, in case he had forgotten during his attack of the sleeping-beauties.

'Our strong man needs a lot of concentrated nourishment to keep up his strength,' the big-eared man said, tossing him a huge slice of applecrumf and half a dozen scrummits. 'But as for me, I say *manners* before a meal. Let me introduce myself. I am Arthur, and this ravishing green-haired beauty is my dear wife, Martha,' (the green-haired woman and the big-eared man gave each other loving glances) 'and we are the owners and head clowns of the Wonder Show. After all, when you wake up and find yourself beyond the edge of the known universe with your heart broken and happiness destroyed, the best thing to do is to make others happy ... but I can't go into all that right now.

'Now that rag-tag tangle of red-noses over there is our Clown Company.' ('Pies! Pies! Pies!' the Clown Company were muttering softly to one another, as they closed in around the food funnel.) 'The silver people flopping out of the safety net are the Hirondelles, swallows of the trapeze, and this fellow with the ginger hair bouncing up to us is Ferdinando the Fire-eater, while over there, shaking the cosmic dust out of their trombones, is the Wonder Show band.'

'I'm starving . . . starving!' declared Ferdinando the Fire-eater. 'Please, please, give me a box of matches, a shovelful of red-hot coals, and a few pine logs.'

Jason read the menu anxiously.

'There aren't any,' he said.

'Give me a double-pepper pie, then,' Ferdinando sighed. 'That'll be a lot better than nothing. Quickly, before everyone else wakes up and starts wanting one, too.'

By now, more and more people were staggering up, one and all crying out for food in large quantities. Some of them were so hungry they twisted themselves into circles and came rolling towards the food funnel at great speed, while others scurried forward, upside down, running on the tips of their fingers. A small troop of men and women in spangled tights skirmished up, weaving in and out of each other, tossing wine glasses, tennis racquets, glass balls and cricket bats into the air, catching them and then tossing them again. Others came striding up on huge stilts which were hidden by billowing skirts and long, patched trousers.

It was obvious that, after an attack of the sleeping-beauties, what people absolutely *had* to have immediately (if not sooner) were assorted pies, large helpings of grabfabbit, and chuckle-berry ice-cream. It was no use trying to explain anything to anyone about anything until after they had been fed.

'More jokes!' exclaimed Delphinium, her own mouth full, nudging Jason who told joke after joke. The air grew warmer and more summery, and suddenly it was like a picnic, there in the ring of empty seats. People wolfed down pies, skudge, scrummits, grabfabbit, crambo and other delicacies at an alarming rate, but the faithful food funnel did its duty nobly, and there was plenty for everyone.

'But what's been going on here?' asked Jason at last, after the circus people had quietened down a little. 'Where have you all been? People have been searching for the Wonder Show in every direction all over the known universe, and even in parts of the unknown universe, ever since you went missing on the way to the Piecrust Galaxy. And that was more than a year ago.'

'A year? A whole year?' exclaimed Martha. 'It seems but yesterday that we were coming to the end of a particularly difficult performance, and suddenly here we are, wide awake and starving, only to find we've been missing for a year.'

'Everyone will have forgotten us,' cried Ferdinando, brushing the crumbs of his fourth double-pepper pie from his waistcoat.

'No! Everyone *remembers* you!' Delphinium reassured them. 'They want you back again, and there's a huge reward for anyone who finds you. For Jason and me, that is, because we're the finders − no doubt about that. But how did you . . . every single one of you . . . fall asleep, and how long have you been sleeping?'

'It's one of the most mysterious of all the

many mysteries of the universe,' said Arthur, waggling his huge ears. 'The short answer is that I'm not too sure.' His face lit up like a computer screen that has suddenly been turned on. 'I know! I'll lightly sketch in our life story, in case something useful might come out of it. Bells might ring! It is a tale of deep heartbreak and sorrowful triumph . . .'

'I'll tell it,' said Martha firmly, and the clowns, stilt-walkers, tightrope artists, tumblers and jugglers, along with the fire-eater and the strong man, clustered around to listen closely to this particular life story, just as if they had never heard it before.

27

Life Story Three

'After our tragedy (which we can't bear to talk about in any detail), Arthur and I found we had been exploded through hyperspace deep into the unknown universe. In fact, we had landed on a very strange planet ... a planet devoted to fun. Imagine it! There we were on a fun planet that nobody in the known universe was aware of, and both of us with breaking hearts.'

'We decided to work,' said Martha. 'Hard work helps soothe a broken heart. Of course, we planned to make our way back to the centre of things. But how? We had no money ... no skip-ship ... nothing, except our warm, if severely shattered hearts, and our good sense of humour.'

'We actually had one sense of humour each,'

said Arthur, 'but we decided to run the two of them together. We would become a clown team, and we would *joke* our way home. We decided to make a career of throwing pies at one another, and it was a good move. There was every sort of fun on Bingo-Bango (for that's what we named that nameless fun planet) *except* pie throwing. Our act came as a great surprise to everyone.'

'Yes,' said Martha. 'Once we decided to devote our lives to light, laughter and the happiness of others, we did so well that outstanding clowns and fun-lovers came flocking from all over the planet to watch us hit one another with pies ... usually *glop* pies. They are the most delicious, sticky pies in the entire universe, known or unknown. Look! There they are, 105 on the food-funnel menu. It's a delight to be hit in the face by a glop pie because you have to eat your way through the glop in order to see anything again. No wonder clowns came begging to be in our show, and to be struck in the face by glop pies.'

'And not only clowns!' declared Arthur proudly. 'Jugglers, stilt-walkers and acrobats appeared as if by magic. Bingo-Bango was a planet full of talent. It only needed someone to *organize* it. That's where we came in. We not only threw pies at each other with wit and

grace, but we did the accounts, fixed up pro-
grammes, made bookings at nearby unknown
planets which we mapped and named ... all
that sort of thing. Together, we launched the
Wonder Show ... the greatest show off earth.
Our fame spread. We bought an old, forgotten
castle, painted it, installed rocket motors, and
transformed it into a big top. Our fame spread
even further. Messages came from the known
universe asking for our help in reviving regions
ravished by the Acropola. Soon we were on our
way, laughing as we came.'

'It does sound like fun,' said Delphinium
enviously.

'It was,' said Martha.

'Didn't the Acropola try to close in on you?' asked Jason.

'Oh, they tried,' said Arthur, with a scornful laugh, 'but by then we had installed a Gummidge particle drive. We were always too quick for the Acropola. People began to praise us, and nobody suspected, unless we happened to mention it casually, that we were hiding broken hearts behind these false ears.'

'You can't hide hearts behind *ears* . . . ' Jason began, in his librarianish way, but Delphinium jogged him sharply with her elbow and he fell silent.

Arthur swept on. 'Then began the grand days of the Wonder Show. Every performance was better than that of the night before. Those empty, echoing seats you see around you were crammed to overflowing, night after night. The parking lot was jam-packed with skip-ships; the ticket office rang with money (sound currency, in every way) from a myriad planets as people fought to buy tickets; trumpet fanfares announced the elevators as they went up-and-down, up-and-down, loaded with laughing customers; inflatable King Kongs bobbed overhead, while the food funnels disgorged Mango-Tango, candyfloss, popcorn, hot dogs and other good-fun food. The Wonder Show started off full of wonders, and then grew even *more* wonderful. The circus ring was a ring of performing stars, revolving inside that greater ring of eternally performing stars we call the universe. We conveyed all the *astonishment* of the cosmos, both known and unknown.'

'Oh, Arthur, you do run on,' cried Martha, taking over their life story. 'He can't help it. Our tragedy turned him philosophical. Let me tell you what happened. One night, about a year ago, we were having an after-performance party for performers only (you know . . . throwing glop pies at each other just for the pure fun of it), when suddenly the meteorite detection system connected to the Gummidge particle drive began peeping. We were about to bang into something BIG!'

'*Peep-peep-peep-peep!*' said Arthur, making a strangely hollow yet shrill sound which seemed to go on echoing inside itself.

'Yes . . . exactly like that! What talent he has!' Martha said, patting his arm fondly. 'We put on the clamp beam that guides skip-ships to our ever-open door, but this time it wasn't a skip-ship we caught in the clamp beam. It was a . . . well, it seemed like a large stone shed of some kind, all on its own and entirely without stabilizers, tumbling over and over in the endless empty void of space.'

'We parked it in our parking lot,' Arthur

continued. 'And when we did so, the door, which had a lot of sensitized tape hanging from it in shreds, opened, and several people stumbled out of it, all walking in circles because they were so dizzy. They were a funny-looking lot, most of them with beards, and they seemed to be led by a beautiful, tall, stormy woman who told us her name was Mollikins. Her story, for she wouldn't let any of the others get a word in edgewise, was that she had been involved in a collision with an asteroid in the Flubby Cubby system, and had been tumbling over and over like that for years, living on a store of nutrition pills and licking the wall for drops of water that condensed on the stone. Where *is* she, by the way? I don't see her, and she's usually in the middle of things.'

Everyone looked around frowning, and some of them called, 'Mollikins! Where are you?' in doubtful, echoing voices. None of them sounded particularly anxious to find her. There was no answer, though Delphinium thought she heard a faint, mechanical droning coming from behind the broom-cupboard door.

'We'll look for her in a minute,' said the strong man. 'Go on, Martha!'

'I know . . .' Jason broke in eagerly.

'Let Arthur and Martha tell first,' cried Delphinium, nudging him again. 'Libraries have to take their turn when it comes to life stories.'

'Well, it seemed that these people were all skip-ship cleaners who had been travelling between planets when the asteroid struck them, poor fellows. They were pathetically eager to be useful. They said they would gladly learn to be clowns besides cleaning our circus ring, driving the broom-machines and polishing skip-ships for people who came to watch the Wonder Show. We jumped at the offer.

'But we *were* slightly surprised to find a beautiful, stormy woman offering to help with the sweeping, though of course we didn't want to discourage her,' Arthur exclaimed. 'Sweeping up after the Wonder Show is a big job. People are so untidy. Did you notice the ring of thrown-away Mango-Tango tins and empty popcorn bags that spins perpetually around us?' (Arthur paused and frowned.) ' . . . not that Mollikins actually *did* any sweeping, now I come to think of it. She carried a small computer and that blue box which she said was full of polishing rags into the broom-cupboard, but it was really the others who did all the work. Mollikins spent a lot of time in the broom-cupboard, but *now* I think she spent all her time tinkering with her computer. Probably playing computer games!'

'She certainly never ever made it as a clown,' said Martha. All the Wonder Show people shook their heads as one. 'She *was* deadly accurate at pie throwing, though she threw rather harder than necessary. But if anyone threw a pie back at her, she became nasty . . . very nasty. There has to be give-and-take with pie throwing. And now, with hindsight,' said Martha, turning to the Wonder Show people, 'it seems to me that from then on things began to go badly for us.'

All the Wonder Show people murmured and nodded in agreement.

'Somehow the fun began to drain out of everything we did. People stopped laughing when we hit each other with pies, and when a pie in the face doesn't bring gales of laughter, there's something seriously wrong,' said Arthur.

'Even when people *did* laugh, they laughed sadly,' Martha added with a sigh.

'And there's nothing more miserable than a circus echoing with sad laughter,' finished Arthur, sighing, too. All the Wonder Show people sighed so hard that things were extremely breezy for a moment. 'So, after years of devoted work, *and* after installing the Gummidge particle drive at enormous expense, we wound up with a lot of sad laughter under the big top! Not good enough!'

Arthur quickly swallowed a small helping of the choicest skudge in order to revive his spirits.

'I used to fly through the air with the greatest of ease,' cried one of the Hirondelles. 'Air was my partner. Yet one day I felt myself grow suddenly heavy, as if my darling partner had lost all interest in me. Down I fell (bang!) like a brick, and there's no skill in falling like a brick. Anyone can do it. Look! Here's the bruise I got – still showing a whole year later.'

The Wonder Show people all began talking

at the same time, recalling things that had gone wrong, and comparing bruises. The strong man's great voice boomed briefly above all the others.

'One night, in the middle of lightly tossing a piano from hand to hand, I suddenly found myself thinking, 'What's the *point* of all this? What does it all *mean*?' Questions like that are fatal when tossing pianos. I just let it drop on top of me.'

'Oh, horrakapotchkin! Our last performance! It all comes back to me,' exclaimed Martha. Her smile did not change, but tears suddenly rolled down past her round, red nose, and there was the sound of moaning and muffled weeping as other Wonder Show people remembered their last performances, too.

28

The Last Performance

'Did people boo and throw things at you?' asked Jason in horror.

'If only they had! We'd have enjoyed that,' replied Arthur. 'If someone throws something at you, you can always throw something back, a glop pie, for instance, if you happen to have one handy. Everyone has a bit of fun. No . . . in our case things simply grew duller and drearier. The lights dimmed. Clowns forgot their jokes, my ears dropped off, every pie missed its mark, tightropes snapped, and the band played out of tune. But the really horrible thing was, *it didn't matter*. The audience didn't even ask for their money back. Tears trickled down all faces, both human and alien, for the Wonder Show now seemed to suggest that the whole universe was a mere pathetic trick with nothing behind it but

cupboards of mouldy skudge, and rusty machinery slowly falling to pieces. When jugglers, juggling tennis racquets and cricket bats, dropped the racquets and bats and tumbled off their unicycles, the audience simply sighed and nodded to one another, as if that was what they had expected to happen from the very first.' Arthur snuffled as loudly as the Mangold, even though he had only one nose to snuffle through.

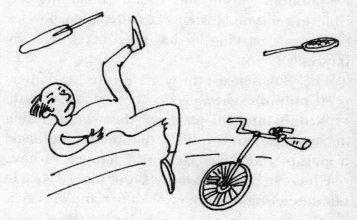

'But we were the greatest show off earth!' cried Martha, slapping him on the back, 'and the show must go on! It *did* go on. Remember that, Arthur! We didn't surrender. Popcorn and crambo bars fell from nerveless fingers, ice-creams melted unlicked, and the cones went soggy. The Hirondelles fell asleep, dangling by their knees. But, Arthur dear, we *did* finish the show. Hoorah for us! The audience, groaning with despair, scrambled safely back into the skip-ships and made off back to their own solar systems. Then darkness, which by now had grown even darker-than-dark, fell on us. And after that I don't remember another thing until I woke up ten minutes ago. Now, my theory is . . .'

'Before you tell me your theory,' interrupted Delphinium, 'Jason and I have something terrible to tell you. Listen carefully. Somehow or other your parking lot has been taken over by pirates.'

The clowns heard the word 'pirates' and interpreted it in the wrong way.

'No pie-rats! No pie-rats!' they shouted in a determined chorus. 'Pies should be protected from rats, and from space-mice, too.'

However, Arthur and Martha looked at one another with horror.

'Not the Bamba Caramba crew!' they cried as one clown.

'At this exact instant,' said Delphinium, 'Bamba Caramba and his crew are all down in the parking lot watching episode one million of *Intergalactic Hospital* with the Mangold (that traitor) who has just become engaged to their pirate queen, La Mollerina, also known as the Williwaw of the West.'

There was a sudden silence.

'You know, it's funny,' said Arthur at last, 'their leader being called La Mollerina, while the tall, stormy skip-ship cleaner was called . . .'

At that moment there was an interruption. A greasy, green glow oozed through the air. The broom-cupboard door was opening. Out of it swept a tall, female figure dressed in sacking, wrapped around in a huge, striped butcher's apron, and carrying a bucket of soapy water and a mop. Her voice came to them in slightly muffled tones, for she wore a large red bandana draped across her face so that she resembled a bank robber or a bushranger. Yet, whoever had heard of a bushranger with a bucket and mop?

'Why didn't you wake me?' she cried. 'I've overslept. I am behind with my sweeping. Tell me what's going on. I want to know your plans!'

For a mad moment Delphinium thought it might be the Mangold, turned suddenly brave, trying to rescue them from unknown perils.

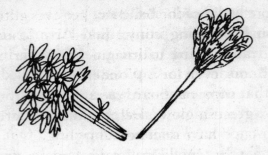

29

Sinister Eyes behind a Red Bandana

'Look! It's little Mollikins,' said the strong man.
'I was just having some very suspicious thoughts
about her, but she's been sleeping in the broom
cupboard all this time!'

'But she wasn't *in* that broom cupboard when
we came through it,' said Jason.

'What do you know about anything, whoever
you are?' shouted the tall figure (Mollikins,
apparently) from behind the red bandana. 'It was
darker-than-dark, wasn't it? *And* you're too short
to see much! *And*, anyway, I was tucked in
behind the broom-machines. I woke up with my
face severely scratched by broom-bristles. That's
why I've been forced to wear this handkerchief
thing. I must protect those painful scratches.'

Over the top of the bandana her eyes glittered with fury at being contradicted by Jason. It was certainly hard to imagine her offering to sweep floors, even for a Wonder Show.

'The broom cupboard was lit up by that greasy, greenish glow,' Delphinium muttered to Jason. 'We'd have seen her all right.'

'Now, now, Mollikins!' said Martha, frowning as sternly as a clown with a huge smile *can* frown. 'Don't be grumpy! We're all just waking up and trying to weave the broken threads of our lives together once more.'

'And finding out what has been going on while we were having our nap,' Arthur added. 'Mollikins, it seems we've been taken over by pirates led by Bamba Caramba and La Mollerina, whoever she might happen to be.'

'La Mollerina?' cried Mollikins, as if she couldn't believe such ignorance. 'Why, she's the one who ought to be Queen of the Universe. Well, I mean she *says* she ought to be Q of the U and, as she's supremely beautiful, and knows absolutely everything about every single thing worth knowing about, she's probably right.'

'Well, she's not going to be Q of our U, which is to say our Wonder Show. She's not even going to be Q of the P, which is to say our parking lot,' said Martha. 'A small, firm battle will soon put this La Mollerina back in the West where she apparently belongs.'

'The West is too small for anyone as wonderful as La Mollerina,' exclaimed Mollikins, squinting furtively at her watch. The Wonder Show people (and Jason and Delphinium, too), all stared hopefully towards Arthur and Martha. Arthur was frowning.

'Unfortunately, all our ray guns and laser swords were stored in the ticket office,' he said doubtfully.

'Come off it, Arthur! We don't need a lot of ray guns,' Martha declared. 'We're clowns, Arthur, *clowns*, not mere commandos. Let's arm ourselves with *clown* weapons! Glop pies.'

The clowns burst into laughter and cries of joy.

'You're not going to throw glop pies around

that parking lot after I've just cleaned it,' cried Mollikins. 'I forbid it!'

'It's actually very dusty,' said Delphinium, feeling deeply suspicious of Mollikins by now. 'A few glop pies won't hurt it. They'll do it good.'

'Well, a whole lot of glop sticking to everything will make my sweeping work unbearably difficult,' argued Mollikins, shaking the mop passionately.

'But, having a lot of pirates slashing at you with laser swords will make your sweeping unbearably difficult, too,' Arthur said firmly. 'Face up to it, Mollikins!'

'How can I face up to anything when I am in such severe pain from broom-bristle scratches that I have to cover my face with this red bandana?' exclaimed Mollikins. 'If only you'd do exactly what I tell you, I'd calm down in a moment.'

'A year's sleep has made you much too bossy,' Arthur said sternly, 'but it's Martha and me who run this Wonder Show, and what *we* say (where pirates are concerned) is, "Up and at 'em!" '

'Up and at 'em!' shouted the other clowns, laying around them with feather dusters and bunches of paper flowers which they seemed to snatch out of nowhere. 'A faceful of pie! A faceful of pie! Pie by the faceful will make a clown graceful. But pirates are frightened of pie!'

'If we sneak up on them now, they'll still be watching *Intergalactic Hospital*,' said Delphinium. 'Oh blow! I forgot! All the elevators are jammed. We can't get down.'

'Well, there you are, then!' Mollikins cried. 'Let's get things tidied up here first. Oh, what a lot of work there is to do.' And she stole another quick glance at her watch.

The Wonder Show people paid no attention to her. The strong man was flexing his muscles, and the band was playing the opening bars of an ancient tune called *The Entry of the Gladiators*. Arthur began conducting them with a sausage. But when Delphinium and Jason saw Mollikins look at her watch they knew that what they had both suspected was true beyond all doubt. They stared at her, then stared at each other, nodding in agreement.

'Jason!' cried Delphinium. 'Did you see what I saw?'

'You bet I did,' said Jason. 'There's no doubt about it.'

'No doubt about what?' asked Arthur, pausing, the sausage with which he was conducting the band held high above his head.

'She looked at her watch,' said Delphinium.

'Mollikins *looked at her watch*!'

'Shut up, you!' shouted Mollikins, aiming a wild, swishing blow at Delphinium and Jason with her wet mop. 'Kids ruin everything! No wonder I can't stand them!' But Delphinium and Jason skilfully skipped away from her blows, with Jason shouting, 'And La Mollerina kept looking at *her* watch, too.'

'Everyone with a watch looks at it from time to time,' screamed Mollikins. 'That's what you do with watches. You *look* at them.'

'Under that bandana is the face of La Mollerina, the Williwaw,' Delphinium yelled, dancing out of reach. 'La Mollerina and Mollikins are the same person.' Mollikins suddenly pretended to be taken ill.

'Oh! Oh! These broom-bristle scratches will be the death of me,' she moaned. 'Grazed and abraised by broom bristles, and this is all the thanks I get for my sweetness and my sweeping.'

'Take that bandana off and let's *see* those scratches, then,' said Jason. Mollikins hesitated. Everyone could see her eyes flash with fury. 'Aha! I saw your eyes flashing very wickedly. It's La Mollerina, all right!'

'It is!' cried a new voice. 'Revenge! Revenge!'

30

A Pirate Mad with Jealousy

Out of the shadows leaped someone who took Delphinium by surprise. As far as she knew, she had never seen him before, and yet he reminded her of two other people. The top half of his face reminded her of Bamba Caramba, while the bottom half reminded her of libraries and of Jason.

'You!' cried the voice coming from under the red bandana. 'Get back into the ticket office at once.'

'How can I concentrate on *Intergalactic Hospital* when I am mad with jealousy?' shouted the two-faced stranger. 'You have cast me aside like the empty wrapper of a crambo bar. Life is a hollow mockery. I have shaved off my beard, and I'm giving up piracy for ever.'

La Mollerina swung the mop at him, partly

as a way of sneaking another quick look at her watch. Somewhere behind the bandana they all heard her grinding her teeth with rage – a horrid, gritty sound. Then she edged backwards towards the broom cupboard.

'I saw you sneak away and come up in the broom-cupboard elevator,' shouted Bamba (for indeed it *was* Bamba without his gorse-bush beard). 'And *I* know what you have hidden in the broom cupboard, too. I saw you grab that blue box after the explosion.'

'What explosion?' cried Arthur.

'What blue box?' cried Martha.

'It *is* you,' yelled Jason suddenly, looking intently at Bamba. 'I thought I recognized you. Delphinium, it's . . . '

'You mean, the broom cupboard goes up and down?' cried Delphinium, barely listening to Jason.

'How else do you think they'd get those great big broom-machines down into the parking lot?' asked Bamba scornfully. 'Everyone knows the broom cupboard is a service elevator. And I happen to know that that vixen, hiding behind the red bandana and pretending to be a broom-master, has hidden something in the broom cupboard . . . something she stole when a certain sealed room exploded . . .'

'After her!' shouted Arthur and Martha. It

was almost as if they were exploding themselves.

'No! No, wait!' called Jason. But all the Wonder Show people instantly rushed at La Mollerina. She flung her bucket of hot water towards them in a steaming, silver arc, then shot back between the rows of seats, and wrenched open the door of the broom cupboard.

The greasy, greenish glow shone out into the circus ring. For a moment, they all saw the broom-machines standing stiffly to attention, their great revolving brooms raised high, ready to sweep into action at the press of a button. And there, above the broom-machines, dangled the loathsome chrysalises, writhing horribly in the green light. Though the Wonder Show people were in hot pursuit, the sight of the chrysalises caused them to recoil in horror. Even Delphinium and Jason, who had seen those very chrysalises only a short time earlier, were shocked, for they already seemed so much bigger, and so much more slimy, than before.

'Catch me if you can!' screamed La Mollerina. 'All the other elevators are totally jammed, and I'm going to jam this one when I'm back in the parking lot. Soon . . . soon it will be darker-than-dark again! And as for you, Bamba . . . now I see you without your beard, your

magic has totally gone. You're going to be stuck up here with these stupid clowns for ever! Ha! Ha! Ha!'

Arthur and Martha, recovering from their moment of chrysalis-shock, charged forward. But the door was closing, and a moment later the broom cupboard could be heard humming its way back to the parking lot. As it vanished, a small bridge automatically folded down out of the wall across the elevator shaft leading from the Wonder Ring to the corridor beyond.

'She's escaped. Now, we're in deep trouble!' shouted Bamba Caramba.

'*Why* does she keep looking at her watch?' Delphinium asked breathlessly. 'Something terrible is about to happen at any moment and we don't know what it is.'

'Delphinium's right!' said Jason. He turned to Bamba. 'Don't you recognize me? It's *me*, Brockley – your baby brother, Jason. I forgive you for deserting me. And now let's catch La Mollerina as quickly as we can. But how? The elevators are jammed.'

'Jason?' cried Bamba-Brockley. 'Is it really you? But *I* didn't desert you. You deserted *me*.'

'I did not,' said Jason. 'I was carried off by that superintendent, and you ran in the opposite direction.'

'We're arguing already,' cried Bamba-Brockley, smiling joyfully. 'That *proves* we're brothers.'

But Delphinium interrupted the family reunion with one of her brilliant ideas.

'The ferris wheel!' she yelled. 'We came up by ferris wheel; we can go down by it. Then we'll unjam the elevators, and everyone else will be able to come down, too.'

Immediately, there was a rush for the bridge leading to the passage on the other side of the broom-cupboard elevator-shaft. Questions were fired, like ray guns, as they ran.

'Did you hear what Bamba (I mean,

Brockley) said about a sealed room exploding?' Delphinium murmured to Jason.

'Are you really my long-lost little brother?' Bamba-Brockley cried on the other side.

'Will we ever bring the Wonder Show back to its past glory?' mused Arthur, rushing along as fast as his big shoes allowed.

'What were those things *dangling* in the broom cupboard?' the fire-eater muttered nervously. 'They looked awful!'

'Moths!' Martha shouted over her shoulder, trying to reassure him. 'First, we'll cut La Mollerina down to size, and then we'll disinfect the broom cupboard.'

Over the echoing elevator-shaft charged the Wonder Show people, following Arthur and Martha, who were following Delphinium and Jason. The band played *The Entry of the Gladiators* as they ran, and Brockley trailed behind everyone else, soaking wet, and still whinging, every now and then, over his broken engagement.

'I'm glad to be a big brother again,' he cried. 'No more falling-in-love for me! I offered to wear a false nose . . . right here beside my real one,' he complained, 'but *she* said false noses were for fools.' There was an angry roar from the clowns at this insult to false noses. 'She said, if I didn't stop bothering her she'd cut my only nose off with my own sword. I wish I hadn't become a pirate. I wish I'd stayed at home, merely reading pirate stories and taking good care of you, Jason.'

'I can take care of myself now,' explained Jason hastily. 'I'm a library with a special joke section.' But at that moment the strong man and Ferdinando pushed Brockley to one side in the race for the trapdoor over the ferris wheel, and one or two circus people ran over him.

Now that fun-energy had been restored to the Wonder Show system, the trapdoor passage was brightly lit, and suddenly music came bursting out in front of them as well as from the band behind. It rose through the open trapdoor, beyond which they could all see the ferris wheel, still spinning round and round, but now flashing with lights and resounding with music.

'Lower us through that trapdoor,' cried Delphinium, 'and drop us into the ferris-wheel seats as they whizz under us. Quickly! Or it'll be too late.'

'Let *me* go!' wailed Brockley, jumping up and down behind the ring of circus people. 'I must protect my baby brother from dangerous things.'

'I like dangerous things,' Jason cried back as Arthur seized him, and Martha seized Delphinium, lowering them carefully through the open trapdoor. And now Delphinium saw that both Arthur and Martha had other, smaller smiles hidden inside their painted ones. Though these smiles were almost blotted out with scarlet paint, Delphinium knew at once that these were their true smiles, and her heart lifted, for, though the true smiles had something a little sad about them, they were warm and hopeful, as well.

'Now!' said Martha. Delphinium and Jason dropped down into the ferris-wheel seats so easily they barely even rocked them.

'Look at that! Born Wonder Show material!' Delphinium heard Arthur say to Martha as the ferris wheel whizzed her away from them, and although things were so remarkably busy, she was still able to feel delighted.

'If we ever get out of this trouble I'm going to join the Wonder Show,' she said to Jason.

'So am I,' said Jason. 'I'm glad to have found Brockley again, but he's not going to boss *me* around any more.'

'Jason,' cried Delphinium, 'do you think, perhaps, jokes are as real as accidents and adventures? Do you think the whole universe is secretly winking and laughing at us? Oh! We're nearly at the bottom. Let's jump!'

'You're not supposed to jump off a moving ferris wheel,' Jason replied, leaping as hard as he could, all the same. They landed together, rolling over and over, back in the Wonder Show parking lot once more.

By now, thanks to all the joke-telling up in the circus ring, the parking lot was much lighter and brighter, and all sorts of side-shows had become visible in between the skip-ship parking slots: merry-go-rounds, chair-o-planes, springs that shoot you up to the ceiling if you bounce on them, and little mechanical space ships that shot around, banging into one another, before springing off in every direction.

'We'll be able to have free rides on everything once our great victory over the pirates is over,' Delphinium exclaimed – quite entranced, in spite of herself. 'Look! There's La Mollerina, just strolling towards the ticket office. She doesn't realize that we've managed to come down by ferris wheel.'

La Mollerina had jammed the broom-cupboard door open with her bucket, and was now walking across the parking lot in an unhurried way, taking off her red bandana as she went. Her electric blue hair suddenly sprang free and flashed out like lightning. As she arrived at the ticket office, she glanced at her watch, then flung the door wide.

'Prepare to receive boarders!' they heard her shouting. 'We'll catch them, keelhaul them, scupper them, and make them walk the plank.'

But Delphinium and Jason, who had been scuttling around the edge of the parking lot, had almost reached the elevators.

31

The Battle Begins

The elevator doors were still jammed open. Jason and Delphinium hastily snatched away the foam-rubber hamburger, the strings of rubber sausages, the plastic dinosaur, the false pies and all other obstructions. The doors sighed gratefully as they closed at last. There was a sudden burst of music. An unexpected fanfare of trumpets rang out overhead, and then the elevators began humming upwards.

'Trumpets! They might have warned us,' groaned Delphinium. 'We'll never catch the pirates by surprise now.'

'Reinforcements will be here in just a moment,' said Jason. 'I think it'll be hard to beat the Clown Company if they bring a lot of glop pies with them.'

But at that moment wild yells burst from the

ticket-office side of the parking lot. The pirates had certainly heard the trumpet fanfare.

Out of the ticket office they swept, a desperate mob, led by La Mollerina, and pushing the Mangold in front of them.

'Defend the parking lot!' the pirates were shouting. 'Defend La Mollerina, the magnificent Williwaw of the West!'

'Don't worry about me,' the Mangold was calling desperately, waving his arms. 'Leave me out of this! I'll defend the ticket office for you.' Someone slid a laser sword into his hand, and his fingers frantically closed on it.

At that moment, La Mollerina caught sight of Delphinium and Jason by the elevators.

'There they are! Kids! Ruining everything for me! Sulking and skulking!' she screamed, pointing at them with a voltabolta, a particularly dangerous sort of gun, the barrel of which was covered with dials and triggers.

At La Mollerina's cry, the pirates changed direction, and began charging towards the elevators. The Mangold, suddenly realizing he was being rushed into battle while holding a laser sword, dropped it with a shrill scream.

'Back to the ferris wheel,' Delphinium called to Jason.

But at that exact moment another series of trumpet fanfares brayed out overhead. The

elevators hummed, then glided open. Out poured
the rest of the circus people, led by Brockley.

'Watch out, La Mollerina!' he shouted. 'A
big brother and babysitter, bent on revenge, is
after you.'

'I don't *need* a babysitter now!' cried Jason.

As for Delphinium, she was concentrating on
the battle that was about to begin.

'Pie in the face! Pie in the face!' was the
dread war-cry of the clowns, now armed with a
huge number of glop pies. Not only that, the
Hirondelles were pulling Tag-A on several self-
inflating King Kongs, which rapidly swelled to
monstrous size and bobbed ferociously towards
the enemy.

At the sight of the King Kongs, the Mangold
fainted, and this hindered the pirates, who were
forced to pass him back over their heads and toss
him towards the ticket office. But La Mollerina,
ignoring his plight, even though he was her
most recent fiancé, took aim with the voltabolta,
firing rapidly at the King Kongs. Phomph!
Phomph! Phomph! She hit every one of them,
and they turned first red, then orange, yellow,
green, blue, indigo and finally violet, before
vanishing into future time. Caught between two
armies, pirates and clowns, and with volts from
the voltabolta lighting up the banners overhead,
Jason and Delphinium prepared to fight – first,

for their lives, secondly, for the Wonder Show, and thirdly, for the glory of accidents that just might turn out to be adventures. Shrieking with two kinds of fury, the funny and the fierce, clowns and pirates crashed into one another, and the battle for the Wonder Show began.

Part Four

32

The Great Battle

As the pirates were armed with ray guns and laser swords, they should have won almost at once. But their aim turned out to be terrible, whereas all the clowns hurled their glop pies with deadly accuracy. Arthur and Martha (Arthur's ears flapping like huge pink fans) led the clown attack, shouting the terrible war cry, 'Pie in the face! Pie in the face!'

Funnily enough, there is nothing as frightening as a clown in a fury, particularly when armed with a glop pie. Stilt-walkers strode around the edge of the battle like phantoms of the upper air, sending stray pirates flying with powerful stilt-kicks, while jugglers, juggling tennis racquets, sprang lightly in and out between the battlers. They couldn't really lend a hand, all hands being needed for juggling. But if a clown had used up his glop pies and had no time to run back to the elevators for more, the jugglers would lightly toss a tennis racquet, and some pirate, poised to fall on a helpless clown, would find himself struck by a forehand drive all the way back to the ticket office.

One or two pirates did try rekindling their flaming torches at what was left of the bonfire, but Ferdinando the Fire-eater snatched them away and greedily devoured them on the spot. As for the strong man, he picked up pirates, two or three at a time, lightly bowling them to the back of the battle. Though they simply turned somersaults in the air and landed on their feet again, they had a long way to run in order to get back into the fight, particularly as they were all weighed down by too many glop sandwiches and weakened by too much television. In among the strings of flags and banners, the Hirondelles flashed like silver birds, swinging down to snatch up occasional pirates, then spinning them around and around to make them unbearably giddy.

For a while, the battle swayed to and fro. First the clowns pushed the pirates back, but then the Mangold, who had recovered from his faint and was hiding behind the ticket office, roared with fear, and the pirates, who hadn't yet worked out what a coward he really was, sprang back into the battle with new courage and determination.

'This is fun!' cried Delphinium, hurling a glop pie which Arthur had given her, and striking a pirate ... (*Spang! Blatt! Squish!*) ... right in the face with it. She was such a good calculator, she never once missed.

'You're a born clown!' cried Martha admiringly, tossing her two more pies. 'When this is over I'm going to offer both of you apprenticeships in the Wonder Show.'

'I accept!' shouted Delphinium, hurling another pie.

Spang! Blatt! Squish!

'So do I,' said Jason, hurling, too, and grazing La Mollerina who was aiming her voltabolta at Brockley. A small circle in the parking lot ceiling vanished as the volt exploded harmlessly overhead. 'Leave my brother alone!' Jason shouted at La Mollerina.

At that moment, Delphinium was suddenly struck by the beam of a pirate laser sword. It was like being kicked by a spring-heeled cow from the !Wow! planet system. She fell backwards, seeing a galaxy of stars − red giants and even quasars. Martha immediately bowled the attacking pirate over and over with a blow from the plastic dinosaur, striking him hard amidships, one of the most painful places for a

pirate to be struck. He crumbled into a little moaning heap, while his sword clattered across the parking lot as if it were trying to get away from him.

And it was then, as she sat up somewhat dazed, that Delphinium heard a wild, triumphant laugh ringing across the parking lot. She knew at once that it was La Mollerina, and she knew at once that they were all about to find out just why she had been looking at her watch so often and so anxiously for the last half hour.

33

The Treachery of La Mollerina

She was standing by the broom-cupboard door, pressing her ear to it – just as if she were hoping to hear secrets that were being told on the other side. Then she burst into a laugh as wild as it was wicked.

'Ha ha ha ha ha!' La Mollerina cried. 'My darlings have hatched. I hear them scruffling in the broom cupboard. Tremble with fear, you lot! For this broom cupboard is now filled with Acropola.'

'Acropola!' yelled every single voice in the parking lot, pirate voices, and clown voices together, with the Mangold's sounding out high above everyone else's. Clowns might argue with pirates, and pirates might go to battle with clowns, but everyone was frightened of the Acropola.

'This is *it*!' cried La Mollerina. 'I'm taking over everything! I will be Queen of the Universe, after all. I began as a mere home-help and progressed to being a nanny (though kids really get up my nose). But secretly I set my teeth and promised myself that I would achieve not just one piddling little moment of glory, but glorious glory going on and on and on for ever. After that explosion on the planet Dwode, I leaped out of the packing case and found myself in a stone room surrounded by pirates. Pirates! They were nothing but boys with beards, some of them with false beards, at that. The explosion had hurled us through hyperspace into the unknown universe, and they didn't know what to do next. In two days I was bossing them around. They didn't even realize that blue box was full of Acropola eggs. Oh no! But I did. When you silly circus people hauled that wretched sealed room into your big top, I knew the time had come. I would adjust the temperature controls on the blue box and hide my darlings so that they could hatch.'

'It *is* Molly!' cried Delphinium. 'I thought I recognized her. It's my old nanny, Molly!'

'Do you hear that, Martha?' shouted Arthur.

'Arthur, it's Molly!' Martha shouted at the same time.

'My broom-cupboardful of tame Acropola

will soon take all silly, smiling, smirking, cack-ling, crowing, clapping, cheering, chuckling or chortling out of existence!' shouted La Molle-rina. 'From now on, the only laughing is going to be *my* laughing. No more fun except *my* fun!'

'You stupid girl! Without fun-energy the whole universe will run down,' cried Arthur. 'You'll be Q of N and N, which stands for Queen of Nothing and Nowhere!'

'What do you know about the universe?' cried La Mollerina, or Mollikins or Molly – whichever she was. 'I've been charming and cherishing those eggs, and timing them carefully and, sure enough, they have hatched at the very second they were supposed to hatch. Things couldn't have turned out better.'

'So it was your Acropola chrysalises infesting the broom cupboard that drained the fun out of my Wonder Show, and gave us all an attack of the sleeping-beauties?' shouted Martha in dismay.

'You were too busy joking to glance into the broom cupboard, weren't you?' La Mollerina sneered. 'Not that I blame you! Messing about with broom-machines is the most disgusting, detestable work in the entire universe. Only a hoddy-doddy would be bothered with broom-machines. I hated even pretending I was going to turn one on.'

When La Mollerina described broom-masters as 'hoddy-doddies', Delphinium heard a curious, hissing noise coming from the direction of the ticket office. It sounded like an inflatable King Kong with a slow puncture. But, as all the King Kongs were bobbing about somewhere in the future, Delphinium quickly realized the hissing must come from something else.

'And now . . .' said Molly, in a gloating voice, ' . . . now my hour of triumph is *here*!' She kicked away the bucket that had prevented the broom-cupboard door from closing.

Martha swung round.

'Let's put on our best performance yet!' she cried. 'We are the Wonder Show. We'll fight the Acropola by doing what we do best.'

Without a moment's hesitation the band began to play. Jugglers juggled once more, tumblers tumbled, and even the pirates caught the spirit of the occasion. Defiantly, like the great gymnastic team they were, they formed a sensational pirate wheel, rolling around the parking lot. Martha and Arthur both began skipping with ropes of rubber sausages.

'What can *we* do?' cried Jason, turning to Delphinium. 'There's too much noise for anyone to hear my jokes.'

'Dance!' Delphinium cried back to him, and they began frolicking around one another as if they were the most light-hearted double-star in the universe.

'Your doom is *now*!' screamed Molly furiously, wanting them to be more terrified, but nobody took any notice of her. She had to repeat it, yelling at the top of her voice. 'Didn't you hear me? You're doomed!' But when it was obvious that no one was listening to her boasting, she pushed the broom-cupboard door wide open. Out surged the Acropola.

34

Acropola Attack

They didn't have fangs. They had very tiny, shrunken, O-shaped mouths that opened and closed like the mouths of sucker fish. They looked terrible because, as they opened and closed, they went in and out as well. Fun-detectors stuck up from the tops of their heads like cockscombs, quivering with dreadful eagerness, though still slightly wrinkled because they were only just out of their chrysalises and hadn't yet had much time to absorb any fun. Their bulging eyes looked as if they might plop out on to the floor, but at the same time they somehow managed to glitter with malice. Being huge and green and slimy, though, and looking as if their eyes might drop out at any moment, wasn't the worst thing about the Acropola.

The most terrible feeling of misery surged

like a wave before them. Delphinium had never, even at the worst times of boredom on Space Station Vulnik, felt anything like the terrible Acropolonian despair that suddenly swamped her. Her dancing feet lifted more and more slowly. 'What am I doing dancing?' she thought. 'Why don't I just curl up, and go to sleep?' She looked at Jason, and saw the same despair reflected in his eyes.

The fun-detecting crests of the Acropola were already plumping up. Their tiny mouths went in and out, sucking the fun out of everything. Only La Mollerina danced, apparently unaffected by the misery that was creeping through the parking lot of the Wonder Show. The trombones and tubas began striking wrong notes. Alas . . . the jugglers dropped their tennis racquets and cricket bats. The tumblers tumbled . . . *really* tumbled, grazing their shins, and banging their elbows. One of the pirates at the bottom of the human wheel moaned and collapsed, and they all came crashing down on top of one another groaning, 'Arrr! Arrr! Arrr!' as they did so.

'Oh,' sighed Delphinium. 'I'm so terribly tired, and it's all for nothing!' Her feet felt as if they were burning and freezing at the same time.

'We're so miserably small,' agreed Jason, 'and

the universe is so vastly huge, and hugely vast. We don't matter. There's no meaning to any of it. Let's just flop into nothingness.'

Sensing their advantage, the Acropola began to advance. Arthur and Martha bravely flung the last glop pie at them, but then they, too, wobbled as if their knees were giving way.

Delphinium fell, with Jason beside her. Looking up she saw one of the Acropola billowing above them, its fun-detector puffed to bursting point. By now, the band had given a last miserable wail and fallen silent. 'Oh, Arthur,'

Delphinium heard Martha moaning, 'seeing Molly once more has made me remember our little girl all over again. If only I hadn't spent so much time doing research in that sealed room! If only I had been with her just before the great explosion!'

'I know, my dear, I know,' sighed Arthur. 'If we hadn't ducked out to have a quick cup of coffee before the pirates attacked, we might have been blown away in the sealed room. We'd certainly have recognized Molly when she came out of the packing case, and she wouldn't have been able to take charge of the Acropola eggs. But as it is, we lost the eggs and we lost our little girl as well. She must have been blown to cosmic dust. And now it looks as if Molly and the Acropola are going to win!'

Then the Wonder Show – the greatest show off earth – sank into an icy torpor, all interest, all pleasure in skill, all questions and curiosity, drained out of it by the Acropola.

'Ha ha ha ha!' shrieked Molly. 'The Wonder Show is mine, all mine! What a jumping-off place for the rest of the universe.'

But the Wonder Show wasn't hers – not quite!

35

Not Quite!

One question, one completely new question, had suddenly leaped into Delphinium's mind, burning on even after being blown out, just like the flame of a trick candle. 'What was that?' thought Delphinium. 'What was that about the sealed room and the great explosion? What was that about being in the cafeteria, not the sealed room? What was that about a little girl who might have been blown to cosmic dust?'

36

Jokes

The Acropola were swollen with their great fun feast, but they could feel that last question leaping around in Delphinium's mind, as lively as a little lizard. They all began to crowd around her with their round mouths gaping, closing and then gaping again. But, somehow, Delphinium's last question couldn't be sucked away, not even by the Acropola.

'*I* was looked after by a nanny called Molly,' she said aloud, her voice sounding as if it came from somewhere far, far away. 'I lost my parents in the great explosion. Could it be . . . ? Could it be that Arthur and Martha are . . . ?' The Acropola, ever greedy for fun-energy, swelled slightly and became more swollen and glossy than ever.

'Leave that question alone!' thought

Delphinium, furious with them for trying to steal it. 'That question is mine. No slimy, old Acropola is going to take that question from me.'

Almost all her power to move was gone. Though she longed to roar and rant and rave at them, all she could do was roll over and bang on the floor with her knuckles.

Knock! Knock!

'Knock! Knock!' gasped a faint, frail voice, sounding as if it came out of a mouth stuffed full of old socks and elephant hair.

'Who's there?' gasped Delphinium in answer.

'Adolph.'

'Adolph who?'

'Adolph ball hit me in the mouth, and that's why I talk this way.'

Delphinium couldn't help smiling just a little bit. 'What nonsense,' she thought, and as she did so she had an idea for a joke that was all her own. 'My first joke! I must tell Jason before it is too late.'

'Knock! Knock!' she cried weakly.

'Who's there?' whispered the frail voice. It was Jason himself, flat on the floor beside her.

'Stefan!'

'Stefan who?'

'Stefan Nonsense. It's all Stefan Nonsense!' said Delphinium.

It was hard to tell what the Acropola thought of this. Their horrible mouths were going in and out, sucking up the fun-energy as fast as they could, yet somehow they did not look quite as confident as they had only a moment ago.

'Knock! Knock!' cried Jason, his voice sounding so much stronger that it made Delphinium jump.

'Who's there?' asked Delphinium.

'Noah!'

'Noah who?'

'Noah body knows the trouble we're in,' said Jason, and he chuckled softly, though he was still flat on his back with his eyes closed and his shirt hitched up uncomfortably under his black library overall. This gave Delphinium another clever idea.

'Knock! Knock!' she called, thumping with both hands and one foot.

'Who's there?' asked Jason.

'Bumblebee!'

'Bumblebee who?'

'Bumblebee cold if you don't tuck your shirt in.'

Miraculously, she found she could sit up. She found she could actually stand up.

'Stop that!' ordered La Mollerina indignantly from the other side of the parking lot. 'You're supposed to be far too miserable to tell jokes.'

'Well, I'm not!' Delphinium cried back at her. La Mollerina aimed her voltabolta and fired, only to find all her volts had been used up, mostly on the King Kongs. She looked around wildly, then snatched up the mop and ran towards Delphinium, obviously planning to shove it into Delphinium's joking mouth. But a hand closed on her ankle and held it tightly.

'Knock! Knock!' said another voice – Brockley's, this time.

'Who's there?' chorused Delphinium, Jason, Arthur and Martha.

'Jenny!'

'Jenny who?'

'Jennie'd any help to fight the Acropola?'

'We certainly do!' shouted Delphinium and Jason, both on their feet now. 'Tell jokes! Everybody, tell jokes!' They took a step forward and all the Acropola took a step back. Beyond them La Mollerina was struggling to free her ankle from Brockley's grasp.

'In the name of all baby brothers . . . ' he was shouting, 'give in gracefully!' La Mollerina hit him over the head with her mop. But when Brockley took hold of anything he would not let go.

'Get them! Get them!' La Mollerina screamed to the Acropola, and, for a moment, it looked as if the Acropola might flop down, all green and slimy, on top of Delphinium and Jason.

But at that very vital moment Delphinium heard the sound of a motor, and then La Mollerina screamed again. This time, though, the scream was not so much furious as frightened. Out of the broom cupboard swept the biggest of the broom-machines, its brooms whirring savagely. Mounted at its control panel was none other than the Mangold, and he was steering straight at La Mollerina.

In spite of her cleverness and wickedness, she could not stand up to giant revolving brooms driven by a recent fiancé. With a mighty effort she wrenched herself free from Brockley, and fled wildly around the edge of the skip-ship parking lot, with the Mangold, revving up the broom-machine to top speed, right behind her. Showing incredible skill, he wove in and out of fallen clowns. 'I'll teach you to insult broom-masters!' he was shouting. 'How would someone like you manage to be wicked if nobody swept up after you? I'll teach you to insult a broom-master! I'll teach you to respect a broom-machine!'

'Keep up the joking!' cried Delphinium. 'Leave La Mollerina to the Mangold.'

'Knock! Knock!' yelled someone.

'Who's there?' yelled a whole chorus of circus people.

'Barbara!'

'Barbara who?'

'Barbara Black Sheep, have you any wool?'

The circus people chuckled. It was a weak chuckle, for it came from people who only a few moments earlier had had all the fun-energy sucked out of them. But every chuckle helped. As for Delphinium, she actually laughed aloud.

The Acropola were dangerously swollen by now. They no longer looked glossy with stolen fun. They looked uncomfortable, yet they couldn't stop feeding on it. Their horrid little mouths kept going out and in, in and out, while the broom-machine pursuing La Mollerina rapidly closed in on her.

'Just you wait!' yelled the Mangold, turning on the stereo system of the broom-machine, so that fanfares of trumpets welled out into the parking lot. La Mollerina shrieked with wicked fury, the bristles of the broom-machine prickling her very heels.

Suddenly, there was a loud explosion. One of the Acropola had burst. Green slime flew into the air, and then flopped down in a slippery heap.

'Hey, Delphinium,' called Jason. 'I suppose you think I'm a perfect idiot.'

'No ... nobody's perfect!' shouted Delphinium. Five more Acropola exploded.

'Space Station Vulnik's been trying to keep fun levels low!' cried Delphinium to Jason. 'Instead, they really should have been broadcasting jokes the whole time. Of course, commandos have no sense of humour. Did you hear of the plumber who woke up under the bed and thought he was a little potty?'

'Never mind that!' cried Arthur. 'What's the difference between a jeweller and a jailor?'

'One sells watches, and the other watches

cells!' shouted Martha. 'But how's this! What's the difference between a forged dollar note and an insane rabbit?'

'One's bad money, and the other's a mad bunny,' yelled the stilt-walkers, striding through the upper air once more. At that moment La Mollerina slipped in some Acropola slime and went rolling over and over. The revolving brooms seemed to spring on her. Up and over they carried her, kicking and screaming, hopelessly tangled in their bristles. Then down into the dirt-bag they dumped her. The dirt-bag bulged with her thumping and kicking. But as it was made of reinforced polyparrotene, she could not get out.

'Boom! Boom!' cried a chorus of circus people triumphantly. They had to shout by now, because Acropola, overcharged with fun-energy, were going *Boom! Boom!* too, exploding in every direction like slime-filled green balloons.

'What's the difference between a butcher and a light sleeper?' cried Brockley.

'One weighs the steak, and the other stays awake,' shouted Jason. 'Delphinium, what's an ig?'

'An ice house without a loo,' Delphinium cried, and there followed such an explosion of Acropola that it sounded like fireworks.

Now, there were only three Acropola left, and pirates and circus people closed in around them – juggling, turning somersaults, walking on their stilts, laughing and exchanging many fine jokes. Brockley, picking his way through the green slime, made a series of highly comical noises that included whistling, quacking, burping and an exact imitation of musical sausages from the catering planet, Hambone. Big brothers are often good at sounds like this. Not only that, he and his gymnastical gang leaped together to form walking capital letters, spelling out F-U-N as they marched menacingly forward. There was no escape for the Acropola. They just *had* to try absorbing all the fun there was, whether they wanted it or not.

'What's the best thing to do if King Kong tries to come in your front door?' asked Delphinium.

'Run out the back door!' yelled Jason. 'Boom! Boom!'

'Boom! Boom!' yelled the circus people. *Boom!* went one of the Acropola, exploding.

'Where does a vampire keep his life-savings?'

'In a bloodbank!'

'Boom! Boom!'

BOOM!

There was now only a single Acropola left, trying frantically to cram itself back into the broom cupboard. But Arthur and Martha rushed to stand on either side of it. They spoke together.

'Have you heard the joke about the butter?' they said slowly. The Acropola shrank back, terrified.

'Well, I'm not telling you . . . you'll only spread it around,' shouted Arthur and Martha, and both roared with laughter.

'Boom! Boom!' shouted the circus people, the pirates, and Delphinium and Jason.

BOOM! went the last Acropola, exploding and spreading itself everywhere.

37

The End

'We're free, we're free!' cried Martha. 'A million points to the Wonder Show and nothing to the Acropola.'

'It's even worth having one's suit ruined,' said Arthur. He was dripping with green slime. 'Delphinium, you were *so* brave.'

'I was just going to fall asleep,' Delphinium said, 'when I heard you and Martha talking about your little girl and . . .'

'Don't remind us!' said Martha, her eyes filling with tears. 'We'll cry for hours, and right now everyone must be cheerful. Remember, even Acropola smithereens can be dangerous.'

'Well, the thing is,' Delphinium said, '*my* parents vanished during the great Dwodian Flare-up. I was told they were blown into cosmic dust, but perhaps they were simply blown through short cuts in hyperspace into the unknown universe.'

'What!' screamed Martha. 'Can it be? But no! It is too much to hope for.'

'How . . . how *old* are you?' asked Arthur, his voice trembling as hard as Delphinium's.

'Ten years old today,' Delphinium cried.

'It is *she*!' yelled both the clowns, throwing themselves on her. 'How you've grown!'

'I've found a family!' cried Delphinium. 'Jason, let me introduce my long-lost parents.'

'And I've found Brockley,' cried Jason. 'He's promised that he's giving up beards and being Bamba Caramba for ever.'

'I have! I will!' cried Brockley, already looking much more like a big brother than a pirate. 'I'm sorry I was such a bad big brother in the past. I used to think that when you were round about eleven we'd have an adventurous time together. Being a pirate was just a way of passing the time until you were older. And now, I and my friends can all join the circus with you, for we're wonderful acrobats, and we'll have lots of adventures between the stars. Everything has turned out for the best.'

'And who was the hero who drove that broom-machine?' demanded Arthur. 'Never have I seen such a ferocious pursuit!'

'It was me,' said the Mangold's voice. He

sounded small and ashamed, even though he had revenged the insult to broom-machines so successfully.

Looking around one of Arthur's huge ears, Delphinium winked at Jason. After all, nobody else in the Wonder Show really knew just how treacherous the Mangold had been.

'What a hero!' she cried quickly. 'First he helped us to find the Wonder Show, and then, right in the nick of time, he swept Molly off her feet.'

'He can have the reward for finding the Wonder Show,' cried Jason. 'Now I've found my big brother, I don't need the reward as much as I thought I did.'

'Kirfizzlplutz! I may have behaved a shade unwisely in the recent past,' the Mangold confessed, cheering up, 'but if I am rich, I'll hire people to be brave for me. And in the meantime, I'll sweep up all this slime. After all, I *am* a broom-master.'

'It might come alive again,' said Delphinium. 'Remember when it was shot into smithereens by the commandos . . . '

'I've been watching it, but it hasn't so much as twitched,' said Arthur. 'You know, I believe that Acropola which have burst through absorbing too much fun-energy actually *stay* burst. I don't think they *can* reconstitute.' They all stared intently at the slime, but there certainly wasn't an itch or a twitch left in it.

'Sweep it on top of Molly,' suggested Martha. Shrill screams of rage, together with a lot of sneezing and coughing, came from the dirt-bag of the broom-machine. But Molly was not at all sorry for her wickedness.

'You wait!' she yelled. 'I'll escape from this dirt-bag. I'll escape from any prison-planet on which you put me. I am La Mollerina, and I'm going to be Q of the U one way or another. Then you'll all be sorry!'

'I was never entirely happy about being engaged to her,' said the Mangold. 'It all happened so suddenly. And when I heard her speak as she did about broom-machines, well, it was all over and done with as far as I was concerned.'

Delphinium felt wonderfully light-hearted.

'We won! We won!' she cried happily. 'The universe was on our side all the time. It's our mother, father and big brother. It's a Wonder Show itself, a star circus of jugglers, acrobats and clowns. It's as if grand things and funny things wind up holding hands and dancing.'

'You wait!' yelled Molly. 'Don't forget I'm part of the universe, too.' But nobody was listening to Molly.

The band struck up its circus tune again, and everyone began doing what they did best.

Look! They are dancing with the story. The Mangold handles his broom-machine in an amazingly masterful fashion. The strong man lifts Delphinium in one hand and Jason in the other. Everyone cheers and claps, and nobody sees Molly escape from the dirt-bag of the broom machine and run off to the skip-ship *Dragonfly*. Jason and Delphinium stand, one on each enormous palm, tottering a little, for nothing is ever perfectly safe. But they don't fall . . . not this time. Though the universe is not quite balanced, it is balanced enough for most of us. *Whooosh!* Off goes the skip-ship *Dragonfly*! Molly has escaped and soon she will be causing trouble in some other part of the known universe. But nobody notices. Arthur holds high his dark-blue hoop with the winking sun and smiling moon.

It is Delphinium's tenth birthday.

'Happy birthday to me!' she sings, diving through the blue hoop. 'Happy birthday to me.' Martha catches her on the other side, and hugs her. 'Here's to jokes and adventures! Happy birthday to me!'

Jason joins in. The whole circus begins singing the Happy Birthday song to her. And, as she listens, smiling, Delphinium believes the Wonder Show, the story, and indeed the whole universe, is offering her a moment of glory.